SISTERS OF THE WILD SAGE

A WEIRD WESTERN COLLECTION

NICOLE GIVENS KURTZ

MOCHA MEMOIRS
PRESS

Offering New Flavors in Fiction

CONTENTS

COPYRIGHT

Published by Mocha Memoirs Press, LLC
ISBN 978-0-9998522-4-8

CREDITS:

Cover Art: Daniel Hugo

Cover Art Lettering: Marcellus Shane Jackson

Editor: Misty Massey

Proofreader: Weston J. Smith

Printed in the United States of America

ACKNOWLEDGEMENTS

Writing is often a lonely task. A writer sits down and bleeds onto the keyboard or tablet until a story is born. That newborn story grows on a diet of words, plot, and conflict. The stories in this collection grew up, went out into the world, and were welcomed into magazines, anthologies, and collections. It is with appreciation to those gatekeepers and editors who saw the potential in these stories and introduced them to their readers. Specifically, I would like to thank David Lee Summers who read my very first weird westerns, edited them, and gave them a publication in his Tales of the Talisman magazine. David Boop, editor and author, who gave me my first professional weird western sale in Baen's Straight Outta Tombstone. Other editors who took my quirky love for strange western stories and shared them include, but are not limited to, Misty Massey, Emily Leverett, David Riley, Margaret S. McGraw, John G. Hartness, Milton Davis, and many others. Of course, none of the stories would be possible without the love and support of my mother, my children, and my partner. They allowed me, often without complaint, to disappear into the weird west for hours at a time. They sent provisions, so I didn't starve, and retrieved wayward print outs. My partner read multiple drafts and killed some of my darlings.

In 2001, I relocated to New Mexico from sunny San Diego. The state enchanted me and I was forever changed by its people, its sense of place, and its persistence to survive no matter the landscape's harshness. I learned to find beauty in the most parched of locales. Forever altered, like most of the characters in the following stories, I take opportunities to return then as often as I can.

I hope you too become enchanted and changed.

So, saddle up, partner!

You're heading into the weird American southwest.

REVIVAL

1902
New Mexico Territory

Francine "Frankie" Mules was born in a gospel tent. That April evening, the raging New Mexican wind ripped about the pinned back flaps, whipping them about the poles plunged deep into the dirt. The poles anchored the makeshift structure to the earth but allowed enough of the spirit to roar out in hot Biblical truths and tongues. Mother Nature's raging melody of *whap, whap, whap* served as a base for the music spilling out of the tent.

In the tent's rear, Frankie's momma, Jet, squatted and then collapsed to her knees, sweating through the anointing oil and the deacon's palm print on her forehead. She ignored the pangs of Eve's curse, choosing instead to mutter prayers through cracked lips and cotton mouth. Once her water broke, a shot of pink, watery rivulets raced down her thighs and into the dry earth. Jet's sister, Joan, buried her fingernails into her flesh of her arm, and prayed for Jesus to take over.

Before anyone could fetch the doctor down in Wild Sage, Frankie slipped out, smacking the hardened desert floor with a *thack*. Joan scooped her up all slippery and pink, mouth balled up as if sucking on the already sour air of life. Joan took out her hunting knife with one hand, and severed Frankie's attachment to Jet, figuratively and physically. Being part of some traveling revival, fetchin' and singin' for white folks wasn't the life Lincoln wanted for freed slaves. It wouldn't do for her niece neither. She clutched the baby tight with determination. *Not this one. Not no more.*

"Joanie, give 'er here..." Jet reached out with shaking hands and pained eyes.

"We done talked about this." Joan steeled her bleating heart. She'd never be able to understand how others found the iciness to break up families and snatch babes from mommas without emotion. It filled her with dread and unease. Her heart pounded and the roaring in her ears made her feel like she was drowning.

"She still mine...and his." Jet whimpered, letting her arms drop.

"Yeah. Ain't nuthin' gonna change that, but she can't go with ya' and that revival. You know it. I know it," Joan said, her tone softening. "Sorry."

With that, Joan set off, away from the tent and the others gathered there to fetch water to clean up the baby girl and Jet. As she moved quickly through the brush, she hugged the little round baby close to her, smearing blood and bodily fluids all over her shirt. "You gonna wail like babies supposed to do?" she asked.

Frankie wrinkled her nose and opened her mouth, and let the world know she had come into it. Instead of crying and wailing, Frankie sang, pitch perfect and like a grown woman

2

who didn't know the words to the song but sang with abandon anyway.

"My, my, my," Joan said, with a small smile slicing through her sorrow.

———

"Ya ain't shut that mouth 'ever since," Aunt Joan cackled now from her spot on the porch, telling the tale once more to a now 18-year-old Frankie. "Your birth was as surprisin' as finding an uncoiled snake in the wash tub."

She smoked her pipe as she rocked in the chair on the weathered and worn wooden porch. The sweet tobacco smoke wafted across to Frankie, seated on the lowest step, hunched against the New Mexican wind.

The cabin had been abandoned by some soldiers. Some folks said they had died in the war. Others said the Apache warriors had got the Anglos off the land. When Auntie Joan rolled into town with a baby and a shotgun, folks shunted her to this abandoned cabin. The town sheriff used to live here, but now he rented out to those seeking shelter. Some wanted her to work in the saloon or in Madam Clay's house, but Joan wasn't living to please no man.

"Windy like that night. That one when ya 'ere born." Aunt Joan puffed, eyes narrowed as she peered out across the land. On a clear night, she could see all the way to the trading post. After she said those words, she didn't say more, but had fallen into one of her long silences. Smoking. Watching. Listening.

The sunset's blush stretched across the horizon. A few mesas broke the skyline, but Frankie could see far, much further than she had ever been. She spread her arms wide as if embracing all of the visually lush landscape of Dinétah in front of them, the Navajo homeland. Yuccas scented the dry air. She wanted the strong wind to sweep her up into its arms and swirl her around before setting her back down on the sparse earth. But she knew even that wouldn't chase away the boredom.

Only singing did that. It fed her, nourishing Frankie better than food, filling the gaping holes that living left inside her. The Psalms revived her spirit, and then she was gone, like she disappeared into the notes, the spirit of the music. Inside her song, she was reunited with the family she'd never met, the ones lost to the sea, to the fields, and to the heels of hatred.

Only Auntie Joan remained. Her momma had died just after her birth in a neighboring tent. The prayers of Frankie's daddy and others did not save her from bleeding to death. No. Those cries, pleas, and songs had hastened her momma's crawl into the grave, for none went to fetch a doctor. Not for the colored woman.

Despite the President setting people free, some of 'em still in shackles—in the head, her auntie said.

Out in the high desert landscape, despite all appearances to the contrary, this desolate stretch was *alive*. Frankie could feel the energy creep all over her skin, raising the hairs along her arms and the back of her neck, scuttling across her belly, making her shudder. The wind ruffled the hem of her skirt, tugging on it as it slipped past. The rustle of tumbleweeds and the whimpering of foxes as they scampered across the expanse added to the desert serenade.

"Zara say the wind be wicked," Frankie said, more to herself than her auntie. Zara was her only friend in town, a washerwoman. "Been stories of the wind picking up folks and taking them off to beyond the mesas. To talk to the spirits."

"Uh huh." Auntie Joan puffed like an old steam engine

locked at the tracks. Unable to push on forward. Unable to go on back. Suspended right there in the desert's chilly dark. The rocking chair creaked on. Beside her booted feet a glass of whiskey. She didn't talk about the time on the plantations or where she and Frankie's momma had run from, fled with nothing but the clothes—and scars—on their backs and hope singing in their hearts.

Songs of freedom.

The West had freedom in big open spaces. Chances for everyone to live the life they chose, not one given by the white man. To Auntie Joan and her momma, it had been a revelation, a whole new world, but for Frankie, it was all she'd ever known. She'd been born here. Her first breath was of the New Mexican air scented with sun, Yucca, and chili peppers. Frankie hadn't known that life before, that life chained to white man's work and will, only this one, tethered to the desert and its magic.

She listened hard for the Diné or the Zuni scouts moving in quiet motion across the desert. They didn't like folks moving into their territory, and as Auntie Joan's cabin touched the outer edges of their lands, sometimes the night brought danger.

The nocturnal hush pushed against Frankie's flesh. When this feeling poured down on her, the silence, the loneliness, she closed her eyes.

And sang.

Quivering at the onset, her voice became stronger as the other voices joined in. The song sailed along with the harmonious others rustling about the evening, coyotes, owls, and churro sheep. All making their sounds, their joyful noise in offering to the night.

After a few minutes, Auntie Joan tapped her with her cane just as she was starting the opening bars of *Amazing Grace*.

"Hush now, girl! Somebody comin'."

Frankie tapered off to silence.

Sure enough, the dirt path that led through the brush and twisted trees was darkened by the long twilight-cast shadow of a person. Who would brave the on-coming dark to travel to their home? Wild Sage lay many wagon wheels from here.

It wasn't safe.

"Francine, chile, you really got the voice of a gospel choir," said Deacon Paul Whitley as he reached the bend in the path.

He grinned at her, as if he'd paid her a compliment. Perhaps he thought he had. Any time men said kind things to women, they expected some reward. A smile. A hug. A romp.

Pale with shoulder-length white hair, dressed in black shirt and jeans, he walked with purpose, seemingly unfolding from the growing darkness. Once he reached the foot of the porch, he stopped short and leered. Sweat poured down his face, and he mopped it with a handkerchief. He wiped the sweat clinging to his salt and pepper beard. He wore a dusty cowboy hat and boots. The Bible rested in the crook of his arm. He also wore his usual smug expression. The preacher was a thorn in the flesh, but he'd never come so far as their home before.

Out of the corner of her eye, she spied Auntie Joan's body shift. The elderly woman was readying to strike—or defend. Her thick lips, twisted and pursed, spoke to her displeasure.

"Good evening, sir." Frankie shot up from the steps. She dusted her hands off on her skirt and retreated inside to let the adults do their talking. The screen door smacked as it closed. Frankie hovered just inside the doorway, barely shielded by the screen door.

He had no idea the accuracy of his claim, Frankie thought as she turned back to the door to listen.

"The pastor been askin' us to come 'round and invite yous to our revival. That niece of yours got a good voice on her. We could use it," he said around the wad of chewin' tobacco.

"We ain't interested in what you sellin'." Auntie Joan rested her pipe on her knee.She blew out a stream of white smoke from the corner of her mouth. The rocking chair creaked in protest as it came to a pause.

The deacon's greasy smile faltered to a frown. In his smarmy voice, he said, "You misunderstand me, Joan. We ain't sellin' nuthin'. Just lookin' to help those like yourself find God. We all God's creatures. The revival is for all."

Auntie Joan eased to a standing position. She casually tossed down the saddle blanket decorating her lap. Beneath it was where she kept her shotgun. With a sigh, she moved her pipe and wrapped her gnarled hands around the gun, just holding it like she must've done with Frankie when she was baby, cradling it.

Frankie's eyes were all for the deacon at the foot of the porch. She swallowed hard.

"I know the way, deacon. We ain't interested." Aunt Joan voice sliced through the sharp howling wind.

"I see how you can feel that way, but Jet's death ain't the fault of the church. It was God's will, Joan."

A distinct rattling emitted from Auntie Joan. "And it's this God ya want us to give up ourselves to? I ain't gonna live beneath another white man's rules. I gots no masta, no more."

Frankie wasn't fooled by Deacon Paul's pious invitation. The expectation in his eyes when he first saw Frankie on the porch had conveyed something other than God's will. It made Frankie's skin crawl. She tried to control her labored breathing. How would Auntie Joan deal with the deacon's trespass of evil? She couldn't see her auntie's face, but the deacon could.

Deacon Paul's lips peeled back like a wild fox faced with a foe. "I see."

"I hope ya do." Auntie Joan stroked the gun in her lap. "We appreciate ya comin' round to see about our souls. Now, best ya get goin'."

Deacon Paul nodded, tucked his ible under his arm, and turned to leave. He stopped and looked back. Perhaps he could see Frankie's outline through the heavy screen door. He grinned, wide and without mirth.

"Good evening, Miss Frankie." He tipped his cowboy hat in her direction.

"Ya best be on ya way, deacon." The calmness Aunt Joan projected fractured in that moment. Her grip on the gun tightened.

"Ma'am." He nodded once more and proceeded back the way he'd come. His boots crunched the dirt beneath his feet. A few moments later, Frankie heard the soft whinnying of his horse.

"Auntie, what killed my momma?" Frankie asked, her voice soft against the velvety night, small as it pushed through the tiny screen mesh.

"Pride. Pride kilt your momma."

The rocking chair's creaking started once more. Frankie melted back into the cabin. The night settled back into the sweet scent of tobacco and the soft humming just beneath the wind's unsettled howling.

———

Joan's teeth ached from gripping her pipe. She watched Deacon Paul slither round the bend. Pride. Jet wouldn't hear of leaving that damn revival tent alone. All cause some good-looking man had a sultry and seducing voice.

Joan rocked, the creaking piercing the blanket of evening chill. Her hands ached, and she rubbed them beneath the scratchy saddle blanket. Jet loved that man, Brother Michael. She'd followed him to the edge of the earth and down into its darkened pits, to hear him sing. Joan closed her eyes and pictured her younger sister, sitting up front of the revival, hands stretched high as if catching the notes as they sailed overhead. Thighs quivering, eyes shut tight, and mouth singing with every word by heart.

Brother Michael Mules moved like a beast in heat, enthralling her beautiful younger sister and claiming her as his own. Luring her into the bushes and ravaging her with false promises and fake devotion. He took from her what men always thought women owed them. Joan blew out a single stream of smoke to chase away the cold anger the memory conjured.

Joan's sister died the night Frankie was born. Bleeding to death on the dirt beneath a revival gospel tent, while the others prayed for her salvation. Brother Michael, he of the smooth voice and hopeful harmonies, was nowhere to be found in the tent.

Joan found him hours later in a room at Madam Yee's, naked beneath a woman named Scarlett. After Joan shot a hole in the wall above his head, Brother Michael promised to leave town and never to come back again.

Only one person witnessed Joan's wrath that night. Deacon Paul had been downstairs in the saloon, sucking down whiskies and frisking the women. He'd seen Joan come in with her gun, seen her mount the stairs, and heard the gun's blast.

She'd promised him then that he came 'round her or Frankie, she'd pump him full of lead.

So much that even his white Jesus couldn't save him.

9

For that, she'd gladly mount the gallows.

———

Inside the cabin, mutton stew simmered in the cauldron above the fire. Chunks of green chili peppers, roasting meat, and onions—yes, Auntie had managed to get onions!—floated in the brownish liquid. The aroma stirred Frankie's hunger. Across the floor, a woven wool Diné rug broke up the wooden floor's monotony. Full of color, it also softened the sound of Frankie's footsteps as she set the table for dinner. In a few days, they'd have to go to the trading post to gather supplies, and thus pass the chapel, maybe even the revival.

Could it be the same one that had come to town eighteen years ago?

Auntie Joan stirred the stew with languid strokes. "You quiet. What's the matter, girl?"

"Hungry." Frankie answered, avoiding her auntie's eyes. Somehow Auntie Joan could read her like an open book them white folks be having.

Auntie Joan's shotgun was now laid on the wall by the fireplace—an iron sentry.

"Come on and get." Her auntie gestured with a wooden bowl in her hand. She ladled stew into it and the steam curled into the air0.bn.

Frankie took the bowl, now filled with steaming deliciousness. In her other hand, she clutched a piece of thick, fresh bread. Auntie Joan had baked it earlier that morning. Once she sat down at the table, she sopped up the stew with the bread. Moments later, Auntie Joan sat in the chair across from her. The air hung heavy with the stew's aroma.

With her stomach rumbling in anticipation, Frankie peered across the steam to her auntie.

"Tell me about Momma. Please." Frankie avoided her auntie's glare.

She could see Auntie Joan stiffened. When Frankie looked across to her, she saw the sorrow in her eyes. "Again?"

"Please."

"She was a damaged soul."

"But God saved her." Frankie held her breath, her piece of bread suspended above the stew. She'd pieced together a story about her momma, maybe more myth than truth, from the bits and pieces Auntie Joan had been willing to part with over the years.

"When He did, she turned on me." Auntie Joan took a bite of the stew.

"Turned on you?" Frankie hadn't heard this before, and something about her auntie's silence following the declaration warned her not to push on. But with reckless abandon, she did anyway. She already knew how her momma and auntie had scraped and planned for a better life out West, and how what they found when they got here was flood and dirt.

"She was a southern slave who came to life in the New Mexican soil. I dunno if she wasn't happy before we got here, but she wasn't content. So she did what all 'dem others do. Sought out white Jesus. Buyin' up what they sellin'. Paradise. But it was the music, not that deacon's message, that ya momma loved. It's how she ended up with ya daddy. He was a singer with that travelin' preacher. Now eat."

"But auntie…"

"Eat, Francine Michele Mules!"

Frankie lowered her head and did as she was told. Her auntie wouldn't hesitate to use her hands to put her back in place if she pushed too hard, and when Auntie Joan was done, she was done. They ate the rest of their supper in silence. The seasoned stew and bread filled her belly; for now that would have to be enough. She still felt empty despite being full of food.

Frankie took frequent sips from her canteen and tried to shove the thoughts of her momma out of her head. Her auntie didn't like those unpleasant memories, but she didn't seem to understand. That's all Frankie had.

After the cleared the table and put away the dishware, Aunt Joan sighed from her position in front of the fire.

"Your momma liked the singin' ya daddy did. It seemed to just spill into her, like water, fillin' 'er up. Instead of the Holy Spirit, Jet was brimming with song and music. When the both of them got together, Frankie, they sang so that the heavens really opened up and folks rejoiced. God's spirit poured down on 'dem folks. Speakin' in tongues and shoutin' in glory."

Frankie smiled. "I like to sing too."

Auntie Joan nodded, sadness ringed her eyes with wetness. "You got that from your folks. It's in ya blood."

Frankie retreated to her corner of the cabin. Her blanket and sleeping pallet held her little treasures—the tambourine from her old schoolhouse teacher, the dress her auntie had made for her birthday last year, little this and that.

Her mirror.

She took it out and rubbed her fingers over the glass. Faces filled the surface, blocking out every available space, crowding out any of Frankie's reflection. The ancestors shone from her face, overlaying her own. They felt close. After all, they *did* reside inside her. At the same time, they also felt distant and foreign. In their dark empty eyes and vacant gaping mouths, she saw her pain reflected back to her. Despite this, the spirits brightened when she sang soft melodies or hushed harmonies. Overflowing with lyrical drum beats and strong choruses, her ancestors rejoiced in her freedom. She could hear them, faint in her ears, in her heart. Her music gave them power, but it also gave the restless spirits, peace.

They'd been with her since she could remember. When other things died or left her, they remained. She released a slow breath and began to hum, soft against the fire's crackle and Auntie Joan's rocking. As she did so, the ancestors flickered out one by one.

E arly on Sunday morning as Frankie waited for Auntie Joan to finish her shopping at the trading post where she went to trade for milk, meat, and flour, the town buzzed. A burnt odor hung in the air from a brush fire in the desert miles away. Smoke hung overhead, and even little pieces of ash decorated the ground like tar-colored raindrops. But the faithful paid the fire no mind. People streamed into town on horseback and booted feet to hear the word of God. The wide stretch of road leading through town to the church held horses, a few buggies, but mostly people walking, trying to avoid the little treasures the horses left. Rising up on either side of the street, the town's interlocking buildings relied on each other for strength, just like the townfolks themselves, propping each other up against the harsh environment and wicked winds.

Frankie stood outside the wash house where the smells of peyote and tobacco and laundry soap and the sharp, acidic odor of booze rubbed out the scent of fire. The town reeked, not like her cabin.

Zara Gibson stood along with her, her chapped and calloused hands resting on her hips. A dingy scarf wrapped around her hair kept the dirt out, and her apron bore splashes of mud and oil. Across from the wash house and neighboring saloon, the chapel sat with its doors thrown wide, swelling with the influx of parishioners.

"Revival's in town," Frankie said.

"Every year."

Frankie nodded. "Everybody's going into the church."

"Uh huh. The revival's this evening. The tent's bein' put up now, but the deacon and his folks are makin' nice with the locals by going to their place."

Zara watched her watching the people go into the church and sucked her teeth. "Deacon Paul has a roving eye, girl."

"How come you say that, Z?" Frankie looked over at her, her braids catching the sunlight. She leaned down on the wooden fencing that ran along the porch between the washing house and neighboring saloon.

"Man's shameless. Look at 'im." Zara nodded in the direction of the church where Deacon Paul stood on the steps, welcoming the new flock, and her dark eyes narrowed in suspicion. "That man's got a switch." She tapped her temple. "Be careful round 'im, Frankie. We don't know what be in men's heads, especially 'dem kinda men."

"Stop being mean." Frankie stood. "They wanna save ya soul!"

Zara shrugged. "Mean keeps ya alive. Nice gets ya a nice bunch of flowers—on ya grave."

"Cheery thought," Frankie said.

Zara snorted as she disappeared into the hot and humid wash room. Frankie didn't tell her she didn't have to worry about anyone else trying to get into her head. There was already a lot of folks in there.

Inside her, the spirits shifted around even now. Restless. Stirred by the first chords on the saloon-styled piano pouring out of the chapel's doors. Someone had rustled up the old instrument from a neighboring town. Deacon Paul did behave shamelessly, Frankie had to admit. She spied the good man paying particular attention to the young women clutching their Bibles over their bosoms. Many a round female posterior snared his gaze as it passed by him, his head turning as if it were tethered by an invisible chord.

Frankie crossed the street to the chapel. The spirits came out and growled around her as she drew closer, but she didn't know if it was the heat or the music that disturbed them. Deacon Paul stood in an evil aura, a green creepy color that pulsated around him. The sour taste of warning seeped into her mouth, and Zara's words echoed in her mind. She blinked, and the aura was gone. But everything felt jumbled up in Frankie's head. The piano's music had joined her ancestors' chorus in her mind, filling her up.

She hastened her steps and joined others on the back pew. Deacon Paul followed her inside and clomped down the aisle to the front, the unmistakable sound of his heavy boots and spurs underscoring the hymn. He stood at the mouth of the pulpit, his hands clasped in front of him, legs spread apart, as people found their seats. With his moustache twitching, he joined in with the crowd's singing chorus.

The piano's notes crawled onto Frankie's tongue, bitter and salty, like angry tears. They slid down her throat, coating her entire being once the deep throbbing bass of the drums set in—the ancestor's drums, the drums inside her head, inside her soul. The drums the others couldn't hear. A sharp pressure clamped down on her heart, and the familiar warmth flooded her system. Her body shook, and her legs trembled. Her skin prickled as if electricity sailed through the air. The hairs on her arms stood at the ready. The others shouted out as the Holy Ghost inspired them. Not Frankie. Through slits she peered out across the sea of shiny faces, glistening with sweat in the packed pews, dressed in their best chapel finery, rustling and clapping as they settled in for revival.

"Ah-mazing Grace, how sweet the sound..." Frankie inhaled air, and released it slow, marrying it to the notes, and the ancestors rushed in. Taking over her vocal chords, her ancestors' spirits awakened inside her core. Her voice became their vehicle for escape, their route to freedom. The tendons of her neck bulged against her dark skin as those inside her pushed to meld with the music.

Freedom. Life. Freedom. Life. Music was life.

Their incessant bleating didn't fit the song, and Frankie struggled to hold them back, to keep control of the music. Her eyes snapped open. The church sat mesmerized with glazed eyes and swaying bodies. Powerless spectators. Frozen in the spirit. They knew the words to *Amazing Grace.* They all joined in, even Deacon Paul, even the reluctant singers, sprung up from their seats, mouths singing as if possessed and on their own accord.

This song, of all others, ignited the ancestral spirits inside her into riotous rejoicing. For this one, written by the captain of a slave ship, wrought out of the anguish of her people, the loss, the savagery of their demise en route through the middle passage to the world. The sound of it ignited them, their fury and their joy.

By the time she and the clueless worshippers reached the second verse, her ancestors were threatening to boil over. She closed her eyes again, allowing the power to seep over her, the music to infuse with her voice. Careening forward to the song's end, Frankie let go of restraint and fell into the tight embrace of the voices within, giving herself over to them.

They rose, wrapping her in their love. The comforting sounds of melody lifted her higher. Lifting her like the wind, sweeping her to places unknown. The town was forgotten beneath the musical blending of her one voice into many.

The hymn came to a close, winding down lazily, lowering her until her toes brushed the ground. She opened her eyes and took in the curious glances of those around her.

"Please be seated." Deacon Paul gestured with his hands, getting everyone to sit. He shot a toothy grin in her direction. "That was a passionate rendition that raised the roof."

Frankie sat down and folded her hands in her lap. The pastor made his way to the front as Deacon Paul took his seat in the front pew. Frankie awaited the roll of brimstone and damnation from the pulpit. Southern folks had brought that version with them. She wished they'd left it back down south.

Her skin vibrated and glowed. Singing with the church lifted her spirts higher, to another place. Everything looked like it'd been scrubbed in the washboard. Clean. Bright. Beautiful. She didn't need the Indians' peyote or prayer to become enlightened.

Was this what her momma felt? It must be!

She'd have to go to the revival to see for herself.

———

They'd pitched the tent on a hilltop vista that overlooked the valley. Purple with sage, the valley below offered a strong scent up into the air, and Deacon Paul's soft humming slithered through the tent's opening. Frankie stood just outside the entranceway, her heart hammering in adrenaline-soaked fear—and excitement.

She released a sigh. If her Auntie Joan knew she'd gone to the revival instead of to help Miss Zara with the wash, she'd beat the black off her. Frankie balled her hands into determined fists. She couldn't stand the stale and flavorless existence. Music bloomed beneath the piano's melody and the hymn's coaxing, even when played off key.

I won't be 'fraid to live. An' I need to know.

The humming stopped. Dead silence followed.

In moments, Deacon Paul appeared like an apparition at the entranceway. Dark eyes loomed from underneath the brim of his cowboy hat.

"Francine. Twice in one day, eh?" He flashed the toothy grin that made Frankie think of wolves.

Lanterns hung high on beams chased away shadows from his face. Deep wrinkles stretched across his forehead and along the delicate skin beneath his eyes. Small beady eyes that made her skin crawl and her tummy tighten.

Frankie nodded.

He removed his hat and strolled back into the tent. "Come on then. Ya early."

Releasing a sigh of relief, Frankie came further inside the tent. The disquiet made her uneasy as she found a seat in the back. Unlike the church, only saddle blankets and woven rugs took up spaces on the reddish dirt ground. No piano or instruments, just little Bibles here and there. A few tambourines. A guitar.

Deacon Paul unrolled another saddle blanket and turned back to her. "Sparse, but the early pioneers were thrifty with supplies. Got to be out 'ere."

He hooked his thumbs in the loops of his jeans as he stalked over to her. With his eyes wide, he raised one hand and took a step toward her.

Frankie shrank back from his outstretched hand.

With a smooth fluid motion, he crouched down in front of her. In a soft reassuring voice he said, "Whatcha movin' back for? I ain't gonna hurt you."

Frankie didn't have any idea about that, but instead of saying so, she pushed forward. "Did you know my dad?"

His beady dark eyes glared. "Yeah. I knew Brother Michael Mules. He was with us back in the early days. Boy, his black ass could sing."

Frankie stiffened. The ancestors inside her whirled in roused aggravation. She pushed herself back onto her heels, ready to leap to her feet when the time came.

"Those are filthy words for a deacon," Frankie said.

"Oh no, little Frankie. Me and your dad. We as close as the fingers on ya hand."

He sat down close to Frankie on the saddle blanket. She smelled the horse sweat and manure that clung to his clothes. Her lips moved on their own and she began to hum.

"This little light of mine..." she sang.

"Ya still burnin' a candle for ya old man and momma?" Now closer, he talked faster, more insistent that she hear his words over her soft singing.

"Afta ya momma died, ya father peaked. He started takin' to drinkin' himself blind. I guess he was lonely...weak..."

Frankie could imagine her daddy's days consumed like smoke due to the tragedy of her momma's death. Her song grew stronger overpowering her fear. She shot to her feet.

"I'm gonna let it shine!" She sang out, her body reverberating with emotion, her skin starting to glow, her body a candle whose wick had been lit.

Deacon Paul nodded, a frown creasing his forehead. "Come 'ere. I gonna show you some shine. A man need a woman's touch, ya know? It's all in the Bible..."

Zara's pervading omen came rushing back. The spirits sang out in rage. Frankie released an ear-splitting note when she got to the word *shine*, renting the night. She tried to stonewall his actions, but Deacon Paul was like a many-handed monster. "Come on. You coloreds like it. Always panting after us..." his voice was so low no one else could hear. His voice reeked of booze and chewing tobacco.

She lifted up into the air, her toes brushing the blanket. She glowed like a lantern as the ancestors' song burst forth in full.

Deacon Paul shouted as he fell backward, his arm over his face, shielding his eyes from the burning lights' strength.

"Aye, Frankie! Frankie!" called the familiar and welcomed voice of Auntie Joan a few seconds before her auntie appeared. She scanned the tent before locating Frankie. "Girl!"

Deacon Paul spun around and shot her a poisonous look. "Not a word."

With a relieved breath, Frankie brought her song to an end and collapsed to the ground.

"Ya' all right?" Auntie Joan asked, but kept her glare on the preacher.

"'Course she's all right." The deacon spat, with his cheek twitching, regaining his posture and position.

Auntie Joan adjusted the gun belt around her waist, the shells tucked within and gleaming in the light. "I ain't gonna tell you no more. Don't come 'round mine no more. Ya won't be comin' round anywhere again if ya do."

Frankie's heart pounded in her chest, and her stomach twisted in knots. "He, he..."

"Never mind 'im." Auntie Joan said. Her finger twitched on the trigger, and she pointed her weapon at the deacon.

"Now, Joan, you gonna not want to do that..." He held up his hands, palms out. Pale and sweating, he nodded. "I ain't bothered her."

"Ya did. The last time ya made my sister glow like that from your pawing hands, groping all over her and she thinkin' it was love. I tole ya not to come messin' with my kin." Auntie Joan steadied her gun. She said to Frankie without turning to look at her, "Go on outta here. Wait for me."

"Yes, ma'am." Frankie heard the disappointment in her auntie's voice.

Once she cleared the tent's open flap, the boom of the shotgun tore through the quiet, making Frankie flinch. So loud, the shot would travel for miles. She spun around to the tent. *Auntie Joan!* Frozen in fear, she couldn't run and she couldn't go back in.

Moments later, Auntie Joan joined her at the mesa's edge. The shotgun smelled of gunpowder and fear.

"Let's go! Come on now! Be quick." Auntie Joan started for the path. Her strides strong and her head held high, she seemed more alive—revived.

Jolted by her auntie's harsh bark, Frankie hurried to catch up. "How did ya know where to find me?"

"The ancestors came a 'whisperin' to me. Said ya gone to revival."

Frankie heard the deep disappointment in her voice. "I'm sorry, Auntie."

Auntie Joan sighed. "No, I'm sorry. I should've let you come. Fear took ahold of me. I know you like the singin'."

"I do. It makes me feel alive." Frankie took her auntie's free hand and held it.

"I saw you shinin' and glowin'. Ya momma used to do that too." Auntie Joan started walking again but didn't let Frankie's hand go.

"So, can I start going to church?' Frankie held her breath, her voice sounded small against the enormous landscape.

"Yeah." Auntie Joan said. "Go on an' make a joyful noise."

The End

BELLY SPEAKER

The sharp New Mexican wind lodged grit in the corners of her mouth. Honeysuckle wiped her lips with the back of her sleeve and spat onto the dirt just outside the town of Wild Sage. Morning broke the horizon. She squinted against the shimmering light. All around, the desert landscape changed like so many towns before with tall poles and colorful canopies, exotic wildlife, and strange odors. Tucked into the crook of Honey's arm, Momma Wynn watched with unblinking eyes as the rainbow of tents sprouted up against the flushed sky. Early morning laborers' grunts and shouts broke the new day's quiet. Fires snapped and crackled from makeshift pits. Smoke wafted across the field, snaking across the grounds, seeking freedom.

"Honey! Git over 'ere and lend a hand. Ya know Anna's wit' child!" The carnival owner, Bob Mathers, gestured his meaty and chapped hands toward Anna, swollen and pink, who rubbed the small of her back.

"I'm practicing." Honeysuckle adjusted Momma Wynn against her knee, and then gestured with her head to the doll.

"Practicing what? How hard is it to make that stupid log of wood talk? Git over 'ere," Bob barked.

Don'tcha go over to 'em. Bloated pale pig. Momma Wynn's hoarse voice held hints of anger.

"You say somethin'?" Bob crossed his arms across his round belly and glared. "Eh?"

"Nothing!" Honeysuckle squinted at Momma Wynn and met her glass glare. In a whisper, she added, "Shush you. He the boss. We the workers."

You the slave and he the massa.

"We ain't slave no more. Thank ya, Mr. Lincoln, God rest his soul. We found freedom doin' this work. Now come on. No rockin' the boat." Honeysuckle sighed and sat Momma Wynn down beside her chair before heading over to the carnival owner.

People crawled around—some she knew, some she didn't. Honeysuckle found comfort in strangers. Her dark robe brushed the tops of her boots as she walked. Her steps fell in a shush across the desert floor but shot little dusty clouds in her wake.

Even once she reached Big Bob, she could hear Momma Wynn whispering in her mind. *Don listen to 'em. Don't listen to 'em. Devils! Demons!*

"You walk so slow, lazy ass." Bob grunted and started toward the big tent. "Hercules could use some help with the cages."

Honeysuckle let it go, as her people had practiced doing for decades, letting the rancid bark of those supposedly superior flow from their scarred and marred backs. Holding her head high, she reached Hercules.

"Big man."

"Witch." He rumbled in greeting as he stood tall against the rising sun. Already drenched with sweat, he pushed a punishing hand through his shoulder-length hair. A mountain of a man, Hercules hadn't been his real name. After the war, everyone became someone else, even the nobodies. Carnival work gave them labels, allowed them to become strong men, funny men, belly speakers.

"I told you not to call me that." Honeysuckle reached down for the sledgehammer. "My momma was killed by witchcraft."

"Ah." Hercules had a sheen of anxious sweat dripping down his forehead. A hulking dark figure, he reached out for the sledgehammer. Callused rough hands waved her toward him. "Gimme, *witch*."

He smirked outright, fleshing out a dimple. If he hadn't been so cruel, he might've been handsome.

A cold chill filtered up from her belly, gushing like a geyser inside her.

Thack!

She swung the heavy sledgehammer with ease, as if she had an extra set of hands. Honeysuckle watched the scarlet wound blossom across Hercules' upper chest, at the base of his throat, where the hammer's chipped edge snared his tanned flesh. The red stain inked its way through his thick fingers, clawing at his throat, dark eyes bulging as he fought to breathe.

Round, unblinking eyes took it all in.

"You don't hear too good. Do ya?" The sledgehammer smacked the dirt as it slid from Honeysuckle's grasp.

The icy burn began to recede, and as it did, she came back to herself. Her limbs tingled with pinpricks as if she'd been out in the cold too long. At once, Bob's shouting and Hercules' wheezing screams rent the dry air, and the thundering of running feet joined.

"What the hell you doin?" Bob shoved Honeysuckle aside. "Here! Here! Anna, get the doc!"

Honeysuckle's belly balled into a knot of gnawing fear. *What happened?*

She stumbled forward, tripping over the hammer's handle but catching herself before she hit the ground.

Bob snatched himself around to her, red-faced and spitting, fat bushy eyebrows crouched down in fury over angry, beady eyes. "You ain't right in the head. Git outta my sight! Where the hell is Doc? Herc's turnin' blue!"

Honeysuckle pushed through the thin crowd and marched back to her trailer, scooped up Momma Wynn, and retreated to its comforts. Inside, the oily smell of kerosene overpowered the scents of old tomes and the passage of time. The lantern's soft glow cast shadows into heavy curtains and worn, leather-bound books. She plopped down on the edge of her bed and grabbed a bottle of whiskey from the floor beside. As she fingered the capped mouth, the amber liquid sloshed about half empty.

Just like Honeysuckle.

"What happened?"

Honeysuckle whirled around to Momma Wynn sitting on the loveseat.

The miniature doll with its hand-painted clothing, shoes, and facial features shook and began to grow. The wood rings pulsated in hypnotic fashion. Her soulless eyes widened, as did she—long wooden legs stretched out until the four-toed feet touched the throw rug. Lanky, thin, branch-like arms creaked as she reached out with four-fingered hands. The oblong head swelled 'til it reached the ceiling. Leafy branches sprouted around her head to create a verdant hair.

Her lipless mouth opened, and Momma Wynn spoke. "Nothin'."

"Nothin'! He could die! If Hercules dies, Imma be headed for the noose, and you to the fire."

"Squashin' a bug. Riddin' the area of pests. Nothin' more." The gravelly voice clashed with Momma Wynn's faux cheery face. Somehow it made her words more sinister.

Honeysuckle swallowed to ease her dry throat before trying again.

"There's a big difference between bugs and people."

Momma Wynn's shimmering laughter shook her leaves, making them rustle in the small space, forcing the shadows to flicker. It raised gooseflesh along Honeysuckle's arms and tightened the knot in her belly.

Ever since she could remember, she'd had Momma Wynn. The wooden doll had spoken to her when she'd been old enough to fetch water from the well back in Tennessee, but never had she been in such a predicament as this. With mounting fear, Honeysuckle gaped at Momma Wynn, reclining on the loveseat unabashed. The grinning mouth, stretched to accommodate the now larger face, mocked Honeysuckle's fury. At the moment, all Honeysuckle could do was wait.

"Momma, we can't just attack a white man, even all the way out here! There's gonna be hell to pay, even if Hercules don't die."

"Ain't nobody gonna call me outta my name. Not no more."

"He didn't. He was talkin' to me..."

"Same as talkin' to me."

"But, Momma..."

"Hush now, chile."

———

A series of shouts and the sounds of laborers outside jolted Honeysuckle awake. Through bleary eyes and a pounding headache, she looked over to Momma Wynn. Though still seated on the loveseat, the doll's feet were now suspended high above the throw rug. Honeysuckle closed her eyes and breathed through the thundering at her temples. How'd she read the stars so wrong? Joining up with Bob's Traveling Circus had given her a place to stay, a way to see the country, and money, her own freedom. She peered over at Momma Wynn. Had she really achieved that freedom? Yeah, from bondage and servitude, sure. Although never alone, she *was* alone all the time. Momma Wynn didn't like people, especially those being friendly with Honeysuckle. The doll had helped her ice over the grief of her momma's death and helped her talents as a belly speaker grow. But, the doll had also crept up inside of her and torn a hole that she couldn't fix.

"My head aches. I hate this."

"No, you don't. You just ain't use to what you like." Momma Wynn snickered.

"I know this is wrong!" Honeysuckle climbed to her feet, using the bed as leverage. Held down by her side, her fist shook as she stepped closer to the smirking dummy. The big painted-on smile and those wide, unblinking eyes stared straight ahead. It infuriated Honeysuckle.

"It's better to feel pain than nothin' at all."

Honeysuckle pulled back her hand from where she'd reached for Momma Wynn. The doll laughed. Despite the mirth, it held warning.

"How would you know? You don't feel anything! Just a stupid dummy." Honeysuckle crossed her arms in a huff.

Momma Wynn had a way of reducing her from her twenty-five years to twelve.

"Your bones gonna be dust, forgotten and absorbed into the black earth, soon enough. Take pleasure in sufferin'! That's all there is anyway."

"Just cause my skin is dark don' mean Imma just lay down and die. Yeah, we suffer, Momma, but we live too. We fight hard, but we rise up and live. Imma keep on livin'."

Honeysuckle sighed as the cool springs rose from her belly, filtering through her body, like rushing waters. She'd pushed too far.

"Momma..." She hated how it sounded so much like a whine. "Somehow, you make me feel like I can't live without you, and I'm big enough now to get on."

"Out here folks live by the loaded gun. Only one gonna defend ya and keep ya safe, baby girl. *Me*."

A shudder rocketed through Honeysuckle. Momma Wynn's words rattled around inside her, down into her empty belly where all manner of darkness swirled, or so she imagined. Thanks to Momma Wynn, she could never trust her own eyes. The magic altered how she saw things. Honeysuckle knew there was something beyond *this*.

I can get away from her, but...

Banging interrupted her thoughts.

"Honey! Open this blasted door 'fore I tear it off!" Bob's knocking shook the trailer.

"Comin'! I'm comin'." She dropped the empty whiskey bottle, and it clattered to the floor.

With her head full of regret, Honeysuckle went to the door and peered through the thin curtain. Sure enough, Bob's balding and sunburned head turned to face her.

"Open the door!"

With a sigh, she unlocked the door and retreated farther

inside. If the mob wanted her, they'd have to come in and get her. She wasn't gonna make it easy for them. The trailer sagged under Bob's weight. He squeezed into the tiny room, filling it with the odor of sweat and filth. He got almost to the loveseat before he quit trying to get closer.

Honeysuckle climbed to the rear of her bed where a small window rested at her back. Crouched on her heels, she held Momma Wynn in one hand. The roaring in her ears grew louder, and Momma Wynn's whispered chuckle served as an unsettling undercurrent. The air hung heavy with tension.

"What you want?" Honeysuckle clutched the doll tighter, and her skin grew colder.

"Now, Honey, ain't nothin' to be frightened 'bout." He shot her a greasy smile. "Old Herc's gonna live. May not talk again, but he'll live."

Honeysuckle held her breath and waited for the rest. Experience had taught her that white men always repaid in kind what they perceived as defiance. The pull of the icy blackness welled up from her belly and pressed against her lips. She kept her mouth closed, but the pressure continued to build.

Bob's beady eyes shifted down to the doll and then back to Honeysuckle. "You, uh, use magic for that thing, huh? To make it talk?"

Honeysuckle shook from the freezing cold that exploded inside of her. The corners of her trailer went white. Frost crawled up the windows behind her, and her breath escaped in puffs. The kerosene lanterns flickered in warning. Suddenly laughter spilled out of her. Chills skated along her flesh in concert with the stream of maniacal mirth. Across from her, Bob scowled in confusion, at first, and then took a pained step backward, clearly unnerved.

"Where you goin'?"

The voice's coarseness shocked Bob, and he glanced down to Momma Wynn.

"You heard me. Why the rush to run?"

His head snapped up to Honeysuckle. "Shut that dummy up 'fore it git you hurt."

Honeysuckle swallowed but held her lips shut. Truth was, she couldn't open them if she tried.

"Just, uh, keep yourself to yourself. Ya hear me?" With that, Bob squeezed out of the wagon so fast he snared his sleeve on the door's latch. He cursed and banged around the door's frame before disappearing into the blushing morn.

But the tone of his voice had held warning.

"That's it?" Honeysuckle blinked in disbelief.

She already had her answer. That wasn't the end. No way they would leave her unscathed after she attacked Hercules. Her reckoning had only been postponed. The West stayed wild despite all the attempts to tame it, claim it, and abuse it. A fierce rejection of conformity. This wide expanse of nothing held a kinship with Momma Wynn—barren and unyielding. Perhaps that's why Momma Wynn was so strong out here.

"Imma go out. Get food. I'm starvin'." Honeysuckle picked up her rifle and took a breath.

She glanced over to the doll and awaited the rebuke.

Silence.

Honeysuckle headed out into the yucca-scented air of a new day.

———

In the arid, high desert, few animals stirred this early. Honeysuckle pointed her rifle at the dawn and marched across the open space in search of food. Soon she happened upon a group of rodent-like animals, peeking out of a mound. It seemed some stood as sentries watching out for bigger predators, like her. She crouched down slowly and remained still. Bob called them prairie dogs, and told her to keep it to herself. Although the idea of eating dog turned her stomach, Bob had assured her that they tasted gamy and weren't real dog. Now, she had to shoot one because her hunger was so real even the yucca looked tasty. It'd make a solid morning meal. From this distance, the camp's din punctured the quiet. The aroma of roast meat wafting from their campgrounds made her belly growl and her mouth water.

The wind whipped about something fierce, driving some of the prairie dogs back into their mound. They weren't the only ones on the prowl. Once the wind died, the heavy shuffle of feet snared her attention. Honeysuckle rose from the sparse brush, rifle in hand.

"Who's there?"

The wind roared again, stealing some of her words, but not her rising alarm. The hunter turned prey. A way of life for women in the West and in these lawless times.

A few feet away, Bob and a cluster of dusty men stopped. The two on horseback wore cowboy hats and apathetic glares. Bob and Hercules stood, horseless. The animals whinnied in greeting. They must've followed her, tracked her like an animal through the brush. Hercules carried a thick rope in one hand, and an angry scowl marred his face. The deep purple bruise across his neck spoke louder than any words he could say. That shut him up. The others wore gun belts slung low on their waists.

A lynch mob.

She warned Momma Wynn this would happen. Reckoning would come, and as always with men, so would violence.

"Go easy, Honey." Bob gestured with his fat left hand for her to lower her weapon.

"Mornin' again, Bob. Gentlemen." Honeysuckle sweetened her words but kept her rifle raised. The familiar feeling in her belly stirred.

"You know why I'm here." Bob nodded at Hercules. "We gotta make this right."

The others grunted in agreement.

"You sayin' my apology ain't enough?" Honeysuckle shuddered as the iciness flowed throughout her person. The wind picked up, again, but she held her weapon firm. Her fingers ached.

"Now, Honey, you attacked, hell, damn near killed 'im." Bob jerked a thumb at Hercules. "Ain't no savage gonna harm my crew. We can't have that kind of doin' 'round 'ere. We civilized folk."

"Ask the Indian 'bout that," Honeysuckle whispered.

"What? Speak up!" Bob moved closer, but still out of striking distance. "Quit ya mumbling."

Honeysuckle trained the gun on him. "No closer or she bangs."

The men on horseback drew their guns. At this, she finally took them in. Two shiny stars had been pinned to their shirts —a sheriff and a deputy.

Four men.

Three guns.

Two horses.

One Honeysuckle.

As the rising panic pressed against her throat, she

squeezed her fingers tighter around the rifle, but she couldn't make them stop trembling.

Ain't no man gonna hurt my baby.

"Momma..."

The ache eased from her fingers, and a cool calm settled over her. She sighed as the internal whispers offered assurance and comfort. Nothing to fear. Momma promised she'd protect her. A low drone, a hum of laughter, rippled up from her belly.

"Now, dontcha go beggin' for ya ma. You hurt Herc. The sheriff here says that's a hangin' offense." Bob adjusted his pants and gun belt.

Behind him, on the gray horse, the thin sheriff tipped his hat and spat a wad of tobacco. Thin rivulets of brown streamed down his chin into his beard. His pistol remained in his hand, ready to render judgment.

"You ain't got no arrest papers, no jury or trial. This is still America." Honeysuckle swallowed. "And I have rights now. Not as many as you, but I got 'em."

The men chuckled, then sobered.

"Out here, all this openness. Who gonna find ya?" Bob asked, wiping the sweat from his face.

"Who'd care?" the sheriff snorted.

"One less blackie to bother us," the other added with a shrug.

"Killing me kills your profit. I bring a fair bit of coin to you, paying customers who like my show." Honeysuckle knew her act provided good attendance. Curious people loved her "exotic" looks and the strangeness of her belly speaking abilities. They'd often try to touch her hair, her skin, and of course, Momma Wynn. Honeysuckle didn't like equating her life's worth with money— it happened all too often to her people—but that seemed to be all men like Bob understood.

Your grace is wasted on 'em.

Bob paused and studied her as he stroked his double chins. The others' hard chuckles tapered off, and in the void, silence swelled.

Your good heart gonna get you chewed up.

"Ain't you got somethin' to say, Hercules?" The words thundered, spooking the men.

"Who said that?" Bob asked, looking around, pistol slicing through the air as he waved it.

"Don't all you menfolk got all the answers?" the same voice jeered.

"She said it!" The sheriff nodded at Honeysuckle.

"Nuh uh. Her lips didn't move," the deputy countered.

They looked around, at each other, and then back to Honeysuckle. No one else had arrived. She hadn't moved. Instead, Honeysuckle held Hercules' dark, angry gaze. The voice clearly wasn't hers.

"Oh. You can't, can you?" She smirked, but not on her own accord.

Hercules lunged at her, and she fired... wide. It was enough to force the sheriff and his deputy to return fire.

Confusion erupted around them as Momma Wynn's anger rose. A crack of electricity made the deputy's horse whinny and collapse to the ground, rolling onto the man's leg. Agonized howls joined the chorus of shouts and cursing.

Hercules dropped to the ground and tossed his arms over his head.

Bob shouted in fury and with fist raised, spun to face the sheriff. "Ya almost shot me!"

"Shut up! She's gettin' away!"

"Ma leg! Ma leg!" the deputy screamed.

Honeysuckle ran, scattering the prairie dogs and other creatures as she fled. She'd used her talent for mischief before, but this time it may have saved her life.

———

The tiny fire's flames licked at the skinned rabbit with eagerness. Still daylight, Honeysuckle hunched down in an abandoned hogan, a home the Diné had used as a dwelling. Perhaps they'd had nothing left to fight for so they'd pushed on. Or were too weary of war. Honeysuckle had collected tumbleweeds and wood pieces scattered around the truncated trees to make a feeble fire. After that, she'd managed to catch a rabbit, snapping its neck to avoid alerting Bob to her location. Her hunting knife did the rest. The fire's smoke only spoke to an occupant, not necessarily her. Still, an anxiousness settled around her. Each animal scuttling and twig snapping made her jump.

Full, with greasy fingers still tender from pinching the searing meat, Honeysuckle blew out a breath. She couldn't stay here forever. Momma Wynn waited, as did the rest of her own belongings, back in her trailer. With her fear in full bloom, she didn't dare chance a return without a plan. For now, the fizzing ceased inside, but everything felt just beyond her grasp.

She rubbed her arms, but it offered little ease from the raw anxiety crawling across her skin. Using the last stores of energy she had, she stood and peered out across the New Mexican landscape. The setting sun flushed the horizon with pinks and oranges. Such a glorious place for such ugly things to occur.

But she and chaos were old friends. Her life's map bore

many memories of conflict and close calls. Each time, Momma Wynn had been there, an ever-present pillar of maternal strength. This time Honeysuckle would have to be bold, and her boldness would need to stand alone.

But did she have to do it alone?

Don't underestimate the things Imma do, Momma Wynn had told her more than once. The dummy's protection had saved Honeysuckle, too. Momma Wynn's cold sensations left her feeling hollow like this hogan.

Why battle alone against the mob? Across the flat land, Honeysuckle glimpsed something in the falling light. Almost at once, she blended back into the hogan's shadows cloaking herself in its darkness. The rustling grew louder as the minutes ticked by. She crawled over to the fire where her pack rested and fished out her hunting knife. Her rifle would announce her location to others, but she picked it up anyway. The blade would do, but having both made her feel prepared. She scurried back to her previous position by the door.

The wind stilled and thickened with each breath. A thatch of cacti shuddered moments before the wooden doll emerged. Momma Wynn. Some rogue debris stuck to her hair and clothing, but she reached the outer edge of the yard.

"Momma!" Honeysuckle dropped the weapons and raced out to retrieve her.

Once she scooped the doll up, the cold crawling inside her returned. Despite this, she was comforted.

"Be calm," Momma Wynn whispered.

"How'd you get here? How'd you find me?" Honeysuckle searched the surroundings. No one. She pivoted back inside with her heart pounding.

Stunned, she sat down beside the fire. As she plucked the debris out of Momma Wynn's hair, she peered at the doll's short wooden legs.

"Momma?"

"Yeah?"

"How'd you find me?" Honeysuckle's mouth had gone dry.

"I'll find you no matta where ya go. We one." Momma Wynn laughed as if the question was ridiculous.

It raised chills across Honeysuckle's arms. "What that mean?"

Honeysuckle cradled Momma Wynn in her lap, both facing the fire. Momma Wynn's head suddenly turned 180 degrees to face Honeysuckle.

"I men' what I said. We gonna be together always."

Momma Wynn's painted-on mouth jeered at her.

"What if I find a man I like?"

"Then you find him dead."

Honeysuckle froze. An impulse to throw Momma Wynn into the flames shot through her. It might sever the tethered link between them. Would she wither if their link did? She squeezed the dummy. She just didn't know. One toss and drop, then it would be all over. A moment of hesitation made her hands shake.

With a sigh, she set Momma Wynn down beside her in the dirt. The twisted head didn't sit right with her.

Momma Wynn righted herself and then stretched out—her hair becoming leaves, limbs lengthening to adult size. Momma Wynn became more, a full tree of life. Now, as big as Honeysuckle, Momma Wynn scooted away from the fire, as if she knew Honeysuckle's previous dark thoughts. Honeysuckle couldn't ever be sure. Their bond left them tethered physically, but how else did Momma Wynn find her? Sometimes, Honeysuckle suspected the doll could read her mind, too. Momma Wynn had taken control of her body before, so why not her mind?

At this, a chill skated over Honeysuckle.

"You think you gonna be done with me." It wasn't a question, but a heated declaration. "You want your freedom."

"I do."

Not until that moment did it solidify for Honeysuckle that she *did*. She'd never liked being shackled. Once she secured her freedom, she was loathe to lose it. Although Momma Wynn had brought her success and a job, she'd also cost her. Honeysuckle's life was too high a price to pay for Momma Wynn's temper. If Momma Wynn killed any or all of the men in the mob, then things would only be worse. Momma Wynn's unpredictable nature threatened any chance Honeysuckle would have for a safe and normal life.

"Not gonna happen." Momma Wynn's branches rustled in warning. "We gonna be together always."

"You don't want me to be happy."

"Thought you'd be happy breathin'," Momma Wynn mocked.

Honeysuckle glowered and crossed her arms in a huff. Across the fire pit, Momma Wynn chuckled at her pout.

"Only me gonna save ya."

"I don't need savin'." Honeysuckle grunted at the hard resentment staining each of those words. The boast sparked an idea inside her, but instead of speaking it aloud, she tucked it away for later.

"Yeah, you do." Momma Wynn rose and moved around the circle, closer to Honeysuckle.

"Savin' is for sinners." Honeysuckle stood up.

"You ain't no saint."

"You ain't neither."

Momma Wynn's leaves rustled in the ensuing silence, but she didn't jeer. No snapping comeback. Maybe she heard the resolve in Honeysuckle's voice.

Good. Honeysuckle grinned. It felt good to stand on her own feet.

As the day bled to night, Honeysuckle wondered how long before Momma Wynn knocked her to her knees.

Or Bob hanged her by the neck.

———

The crisp New Mexican wind whipped Honeysuckle rubbed the sleep out of her eyes with one thought. *Water.* Clutching her knife, it took several fast blinks before she oriented herself. She took in the shadowy and strange surroundings with fear pumping through her. The blackened fire pit still sent a thin trail of smoke into the air. It stained the room with the scent of burnt hair and soot. Farther away, between the pit and the entrance, Momma Wynn lay face down in the dirt.

The wind wasn't the only thing that snatched her awake. Crunching of boots on dirt and snapping twigs alerted her through sleep's thin veil to something approaching. With her hunting knife, she stood up and crept to the sole window. On tiptoes, she peered out into the new day. Just before dawn, only a sliver of sunlight provided illumination. Figures stumbled around in the gloom. Their lanterns bobbed like fat junebugs lazily bouncing in the air. The curses sounded human enough.

Darn it! They found her.

She had minutes, maybe, to plan a way out. She rubbed the remainder of sleep from her eyes with the back of her sleeve. As she stepped back, she tripped over Momma Wynn. She caught herself, and she stared down at the dummy. Honeysuckle braced for the familiar belly speaker to start.

No cold inkling erupted inside.

"Momma?" she whispered.

Nothing. Only the rawness of her own terror. A strangely new emotion that made her a bit ill.

"Honey!" Bob shouted and brought her back to the situation.

"Come on outta there."

Honeysuckle gripped the knife's hilt tight, thought about the number of pistols out there, and picked up her rifle. The round space made her a sitting duck. Trapped, it was too late to leave. Swearing, Honeysuckle pressed herself flat against the wall beside the entrance. With luck, she'd be able to take out a couple of them before she died. She'd go down fighting, not on her knees pleading for mercy.

The first man inside caught the rifle butt with his face. He howled and swung blindly. Thankful for her dark skin, she blended into the shadows. When her assailant stalked by her, unaware, she swung, and then ducked into the next patch of shadow. She repeated this several times, extending the element of surprise. The narrow entrance forced them to enter one at a time.

"Git her!" the sheriff howled.

Honeysuckle rolled across the dirt and tripped the second man. Easy enough, since he dragged one of his legs. He fell on top of the other man. The deputy's youthful voice coughed out a groan. The men's frustrated shouts as they struggled to untangle themselves amused her.

"That's enough, Honey." Bob's tone made Honeysuckle's pause.

She stood up and turned to face him. He held a pistol in one hand and a lantern in the other. An oily grin emerged from the dark stubble crawling across his double chins.

"Git on up now." Bob pushed his girth farther into the space and directed her with the gun.

Hercules silently followed behind and squeezed into the narrow available space.

"This is a real shit hole, innit?" Bob barked out a laugh.

Bob and Hercules threatened on her left, the sheriff and the deputy to her right. She couldn't see a way out, but then the cold burst blossomed up from her belly. Honeysuckle shuddered, not in fear nor from cold, but rather from Momma Wynn's full fury.

"Beware."

That simple word thundered.

"Who said that?" Bob searched around.

"My belly's speakin'," Honeysuckle explained. "You oughta listen."

Hercules' pinched and pained expression conveyed his anger. The dawn's light illuminated the inside of the hogan and the men therein. They put their lanterns down in the dust.

"She doin' it again," the deputy stammered as he got to his feet. He held hand to the left side of his head, where blood trickled between his fingers. He'd been sent in first.

"A trick. Nothin' more," Bob countered.

At this, the wind roared through the hogan so powerful it blew off the cowboys' hats. Momma Wynn's power unraveled in the confined area, stirring up dust in hungry gusts.

Momma's coming.

As soon as she thought it, the air shifted.

Spooked, the sheriff shot toward the exit. "Git outta my way!"

Bob blocked the door, and the sheriff shoved at the mass. He failed to move the huge man. Bob didn't budge. "You ain't leavin'."

Roughly the same height as Bob, the sheriff leaned in close

and poked him with his own gun. "You gonna stop me? Didn't think so."

Without waiting for a reply, he wedged himself through a sliver of space and out of the hogan.

The deputy bolted, too. "Ain't worth this witchcraft shit."

"Buncha yella-bellied bastards!" Bob shouted after them before turning his attention back on Honeysuckle. "Welp, the law ain't here, so we ain't gonna follow any rules now, Herc."

The wind began again. Coupled with the laughter, wild and evil. Honeysuckle's insides froze. Wincing, she struggled to stay conscious. Bob and Hercules staggered as the world shook. They toppled over onto each other. Once one man hit the ground, weeds scrambled up from the earth. They pinned the men against the dirt and choked them. Gagging sounds rose up against the day. Honeysuckle fought the frost from consuming her by trying to stay awake. If she blacked out, she'd fail. Momma Wynn threatened to take over, and she'd kill them. The vegetation coiled around their necks. Their faces paled before turning to shades of blue. The men's gurgling faded as Momma Wynn sucked the life out of them.

Honeysuckle staggered over to the men. Momma Wynn's roaring laugh echoed in malicious glee.

"Not again!" Honeysuckle couldn't tolerate the callous disregard for life any longer.

"They mean to kill ya. Let them die!" The wind whirled in greater intensity, crushing the life out of them. Momma Wynn controlled everything, even *her*. Now. This was the time. If Bob and Hercules died, there would be more bounty on her head. Not only that, but their deaths would resolve nothing. She wanted to be in control of her life.

"Stop!" Honeysuckle's heart thundered in her chest, and it burned, hot in outrage. "Enough!"

She screamed so loud, it pulled from the depths of her

being. It shot through her like a geyser, flooding her with fire. Honeysuckle raced to the men and began tearing at the weeds. As she tore through the restraints, not only those from the ground, but also inside herself, she beat back the icy feeling. It retreated with each snap. The yuccas cut and scratched her skin, tearing at her flesh with eager defiance. She grinned at the pain, and the cold recoiled further back into her belly.

What you doin? Momma Wynn shrieked. Panic stretched the words thin.

"I'm gettin' back my voice!" Honeysuckle grunted.

"Let me up!" Bob yelled. He thrashed about, his pudgy parts flailed against his bonds and strained against them. They didn't yield.

Honeysuckle crawled over to her hunting knife where it'd been discarded in the whirlwind. She hurried back to Bob and Hercules and sliced through the vegetation. Covered in dirt and slashes, Bob lumbered to his booted feet. Beside him, Hercules scurried back from her, got to his feet, and fled.

"Honey?" Bob croaked, rubbing his neck beneath his fleshy chins. He then patted his holster for his pistol, but it lay several feet away. His eyes darted to Honeysuckle as realization dawned across his face. He licked his lips.

"Shut. It." She stood up and poked him in the flabby folds of his chest. "Imma go and you ain't gonna follow me. Ever. Got it?"

Bob opened his mouth but closed it quick. Instead, he nodded before walking out the hogan, grumbling under his breath.

After he left, Honeysuckle picked up her rifle, sheathed her knife, and shouldered her satchel. A numbness took up residence inside her. Momma Wynn's familiar cold comfort had gone. With a glance down at the broken and battered doll, Honeysuckle took in a deep, steadying breath. Now, she'd do the next shows of her life alone. It felt both strange and exciting. An internal quiet made her uneasy, but in time, she'd adjust.

At last she'd found her voice.

Her belly would speak for her no longer.

The End

LOS LUNAS

A mile outside Los Lunas, New Mexico

"W hy here in this godforsaken desert?" Nina asked, her voice hard, devoid of emotion, and as unforgiving as the land around them. Her spiky dreadlocks stood defiantly to the wind's hardened breeze, just like her stature. Within moments raindrops fell, returning again from previous showers. Normally, August brought the rainy season, and like a monsoon, it drummed its harmony onto the town of Los Lunas.

Like all people who live in an arid desert, Los Lunas residents welcomed and celebrated the rain, for water brought life. The prevailing belief by people who didn't live in a desert was that it never rained here. It did, just not often. Those in Los Lunas worshipped the August rains.

Except this heavy rain had arrived in October.

That meant evil—evil that fell with each watery drop. The last two days of constant rain had not been celebrated or cheered. This time the water that seeped from the sky brought

47

only death. Hence why Nina had been called down to the village.

"Rain. Again," Nina said, her eyes on the village below.

So cold was Nina's voice that goosebumps popped up across Tyrell's arms, despite his sweater, jeans, and raincoat. He watched her, squinting against the chilly downpour.

"If we were further north, this would be snow. Count your blessings," he said, with a smile.

It was met with a growl.

"Yes, well, to answer your questions, we're here because it is Fate. It has been this way for centuries maybe longer. It's time for things to cross over." Tyrell studied her from his position—hidden by the falling rain and the inky black night. He felt better speaking to her about the things he'd been taught by the elders. Nina didn't do small talk.

Nina tossed a flat stone and it skidded across the soppy land. "Yeah, but that's crap and you know it."

She stood up and her height matched his. She did not shrink back or cower to make him feel taller. In fact, she straightened her back to make him feel her full height. He could see her white teeth against the dark night as she smiled at him. It was frosty and again, he shuddered from a chill. No one could accuse her of being petite. Nina could only be described as fleshy or in polite circles *healthy*. Not obese by any standards, but not a frail size six either.

How could she not believe his words? His words were from the sacred texts, from those that had come before, and held wisdom in their teeth. Had the right person been sent for what awaited in town? Nina seemed tough, but doubts lingered.

"Nina, this thing is here. All the signs point to this town, tonight. If we do not stop it soon, it will be too powerful for us. Even the night weeps in worry." Tyrell spread his arms wide, with his palms up.

"Yeah, I know." Her dark brown eyes moved across the mesas. Her full lips pressed into a tight grimace of determination. "It's out there, somewhere…"

"If we fail," Tyrell warned, not liking the taste of fear lacing the undercurrent of his words.

"I know." Her voice, sharp and harsh, sounded as if angry with him. "I've done this kind of work before."

But had she? Tyrell wondered. Her questions hinted at an ignorance of the culture or a flat-out disbelief for their cause.

Without saying more, she moved down the desert trail, the slivers of fresh moonlight providing some illumination. Across her path, lizards and spiders scurried to safety from the hammering of the storm. The majority of the sky was a blanket of threatening clouds, except for the moon. The heavenly sphere managed to snag a break in the cloud coverage and shown bright and round in its window. It gave the area an eerie feel, as if the gods could not make up their minds as to which weather to induce.

An indecisive god was a dangerous god.

Tyrell followed with his hand on his tattered copy of the book of *Remus* and tried to keep it dry. Ahead, Nina walked down the hilly side of the land, slipping occasionally on the mud. Skilled, she seemed to surf the muddy and sloshy dirt.

Clearing his throat, he forced himself to focus on the task at hand. She had been sent because she was deemed the best, but if she did not believe then what was the point? All of her weapons would be ineffective. They'd be killed on the spot, and the creature, well, it would consume all.

Nina raised her head and looked down the hill and out across the muddy field to the sprinkle of homes. The rain slid off her slicker like pearls, rolling off into the reddish, mucky dirt.

"Every seventeenth year, on the seventeenth day of October a newborn girl is born with eyes the color of mist and skin as dark as midnight," said Tyrell, his voice trembling against the wind. "Tonight is that night."

Nina remained still.

"As this new girl gasps her first breath, she steals the last one from her vessel as payment for entry into this world. Her first death. Thus sending her mother's soul back to the land of Ka'Remi," Tyrell explained—his voice low and deep as the velvety sky. Nina glanced back to him, but his dark skin melded into the night, providing only an outline of his face and body.

The rain temporarily stopped, and Nina watched as more of the moon appeared, shrouded by wisps of murky gray clouds, peeking out from behind her hidden veil as if afraid to set eyes upon the abomination's arrival.

"Tell me more about this birth," Nina said as they slid down the steepest part of the trail. Muddy flecks of New Mexican sludge flew up against the cool air.

Once they got to the hill's base and flatter terrain, Tyrell began, his voice amazingly clear despite the wind. "The creatures are the night wolves' virginal children."

"Yeah, the demons who feed on the girls' souls once they cross over to Ka'Remi." Nina's voice betrayed her disgust, possibly disbelief.

"Yes. When the girl dies, her soul goes to Ka'Remi where the demons devour her for eternity. What is left, the child, is more horrible. Born with an insatiable hunger visited upon *this* world."

"Lucky girl. Hey momma. I'm pregnant with a demonic wolf child." Nina shook her head at her own bitter sarcasm.

The glittering lights of Los Lunas, New Mexico rose up from the valley. Nina and Tyrell stopped to watch from a distance, safely outside the city limits.

"Tell me honestly, Tyrell. Do you believe this?" she asked —her voice barely louder than the breezy wind. Her face protected by shadows hid from him. "The storm is an indication that the child is here. Yeah? Do you really believe this?"

He took in a deep, slow breath, and released it. "At the center, a young girl came to us about fourteen years ago. She had streams of blood racing down her legs and a horrid expression of terror carved into her face. The anguish. The suffering. The bewilderment all mixed together in her face."

"Let me guess, she was one of these marks?" Nina interrupted the wretched memory.

Tyrell hesitated, but then continued, "She had sliced herself, her stomach, to kill the child inside. She—she believed that one of the wolves had visited her in the night, and she wanted nothing of it—not her soul being a feast forever, nor her birth abomination feasting on the those in the present. She risked killing herself to be rid of it. The paramedics were able to get her to the hospital."

His voice faltered and he swallowed the hard lump in his throat. Each time he told the tale, he felt like he was back there again, watching the girl scream and tear at her hair as she bled in the freshly cleaned hallways of the Wild Sage Victims Center. The agonizing screams haunted him at night, woke him with a cold sweat and a thundering heart.

"Of course she believed it, her actions proved that. But did *you* believe it, Ty?" Nina pressed. The moon crept out of hiding long enough for him to notice her eyes searching his face. Even in the revealing light, he avoided her gaze.

Did he? He'd been in the teachings since he was five years old. Chosen, Tyrell somewhat recalled standing in front of the congregation watching the dark-robed elders declaring that he'd been called forth. Of course, Tyrell had always believed. There hadn't been any other choice.

Finally, when he brought his eyes to hers, he said, "*She* believed it and that was enough for me. There have been others, but she…she was the first with such conviction."

Nina did not respond. From the blackened mounds that circled the city on the southern side, coyotes' howls rose as if warning them to turn back, to leave this wretched place.

"Why would they be out in this mess?" she asked.

This time, Tyrell didn't answer. This job drove many into insanity and suicide. How many had he visited in the nuthouse, placed there voluntarily, because they couldn't handle the madness outside those walls? Their minds twisted into pulp by their duties. Too many, that's for sure.

He sighed and started walking. "We must search, now, before the storm ends."

"Fine." Nina crossed over into Los Lunas city limits.

———

The rows of adobe houses seemed to slump as if leaning on each other for strength. Nina adjusted her slicker. Tyrell could make out a dagger, elongated, and pointed in the scabbard attached to her back. She kept her right hand clutched around the handle, her eyes darting around the street, searching for any movement.

Tyrell's heart sped up and slammed against his chest as if trying to escape from his body. A bitter taste laced his tongue and he swallowed. Fear. A familiar if not disgusting flavor. He looked down at the book of *Remus* and dug deep for strength. A worn sign announced the town of Los Lunas, population 3000.

Almost as soon as they had crossed over into Los Lunas, a baby's cries filtered out into the abandoned night, snapping the heavy silence with piercing and panicked shrieks. Wailing.

"Did you hear that?" Nina paused. Her free hand jutted out to keep Tyrell from walking further. Rigid with precision, her arm looked like a board. "Hush!"

He nodded. Lightning streaked across the sky as if to confirm it, too.

Inside the homes, several lights were on. But no one came out to greet them or to yell at them to move on. Only fifteen minutes before midnight, the town lay quiet and empty, except for the crying that changed to outright howling.

"Any chance it's a baby coyote?" Nina asked, face stoic.

"I'm afraid not," Tyrell said.

Ahead of them, where the town's main road dead-ended, lay an old adobe church. Its windows broken, its yard muddy squares caked with weeds, busted glass and plastic bags from the local Wal-Mart.

Tyrell gripped his book and nodded in the direction ahead. "It's coming from there."

Nina headed toward the church, her slicker unzipped, allowing the sheets of rain to soak her shirt and her khakis. Tyrell looked away, for her shirt was soon plastered to her body like a second skin revealing all of her lovely curves and tight muscular body. She stalked ahead of him, the silver dagger still gripped in her right hand.

He followed and put his mind on the task at hand: slaying the demonic spawn. Ahead, clutched in Nina's fist, the dagger bore the symbol of Remus, a wolf being stabbed by a silver dagger, just like the one she held. Legend said the dagger Nina had was *the* dagger. Still, if Nina had no faith, and believed the child to be only that, a child, she might not be able to follow through with its destruction or see beyond its cute glamor. After all, she was an assassin, but a human one.

They made their way through the soppy road, the broken gate, and up the church's flat steps. The cries and howls echoed out from its bowels, as if a set of speakers had been set up to amplify the baby's voice. Nina stopped short at the door and turned to look back to him.

"Are you ready?" she asked, her eyebrows crouched down in a stern look of defiance. She snatched the blade up in front of her. "Ready, reverend?"

Tyrell's face broke out in a sweat, the perspiration adding to his already wet skin. He lifted the book and thought of others like him—reverends who kept the prayers and the oral history of their people. He nodded, unable to speak for his tongue was stuck to the roof of his mouth.

The door's handle turned with a slight squeak. Inside contained no lights or candles, only the mossy smell of mold and dampness, like it hadn't been opened in 17 years. From what Tyrell could make out with his penlight, the place hadn't been used. Like the pews, the pulpit sat deserted, too. Tyrell marched up the first row, and removed his raincoat alternating the penlight and book with each hand as he stripped off the slicker before dropping it to the seat. All of the pews had been knocked over as if they were life-sized dominoes.

Nina walked around the side aisle instead of the main one, and then up to the pulpit. When she stepped onto the raised dais, the overhead lights flickered on, washing the inside with brilliant illumination. Nina searched around, startled. "Tyrell, did you turn on the lights?"

"No," he said, putting away his light into his pants pocket.

The downpour played its solo on the roof, making it sound as if hundreds of fingers were drumming in harmonious rhythm. Outside the busted and cracked windows, the lightning flickered across the sky, ripping the darkness into temporary shreds.

After the last crackle, a woman appeared, the lower half of her face covered by a white scarf, her body disguised in an equally white robe, her hands hidden by matching gloves. With her arrival, the light fled, plunging Tyrell and Nina back into murky darkness.

The woman's white attire managed to glow in the gloomy space. The air stilled around her. Even the weather stopped flowing into the building's openings.

Tyrell's hands shook as he opened his book. "Be-begone, demon spawn of the enemy...Remus demands your obedience, guardian..."

As Tyrell read from the book, the heavy rain increased as if trying to drown out his words. He spoke louder, feeling his throat strain as he lifted his voice higher and higher to rise above the driving rain. The downpour didn't enter, but it didn't stop.

Nina screamed, and he glanced around, searching for her in the shadows.

"Nina! Nina!"

Her voice stopped abruptly as if someone pressed stop on her audio.

They still hadn't found the child and already his highly recommended assassin was screaming her head off. Tyrell raced over to the spot where Nina was, stumbling and tripping over debris and jutting pews. "Nina!"

As soon as he reached the spot, or where he thought the spot was, the lights inside the small church flickered on. A blotchy patch of deep, red blood stained the floor. He slipped a little into it. Quickly, his heart straining to be free from his chest, he looked up to the pulpit. The veiled woman had vanished. Why'd he turn his back on it? *Idiot!*

But he knew the woman had not gone far. She was a guardian of the child. Usually there were three, maybe the other two snatched Nina.

Alone.

Tyrell had to figure out what to do next. The child...the child must be destroyed. Only the dagger could slay the demon child, but he had his book, so he could try to restrain it until Nina could finish it off, if she hadn't been finished off first. Still, he had to try, to be rid of it. Only the silver in the dagger could slay it.

The prophecy warned that if the child lived, she would feed on the flesh of those who live amongst her, turning them into hairy monsters, once a month at the full moon. She would grow and once an adult, she would reign over them as pack leader. She would spoil the seeds of humanity—starting here and outward to the neighboring towns.

Tyrell laughed, in spite of himself, a hollow, nervous laugh. The prophecy had always sounded a little hokey to him, but when he first went out to slay a wolf leader, his partner had been a woman named Cyrene. She wasn't like Nina, but she had not hesitated to slice the monster's throat. That was only after it had commanded its protectors to choke the life out of Cyrene and him. He was nearly bitten. Icy chills scrambled down his back

The pulpit. He started for the front of the building. Nina had been snatched from here. Evidence of a fast, but violent struggle occurred as evidenced by the blood all around the knocked-over chairs. Swallowing his fear, he stepped over the bloody mess and stepped onto the raised dais, his hands sweaty, and his nerves stretched taut. He glanced around.

Nothing stirred and the woman left no trace of where she had vanished or where Nina had gone.

No bloody footprints leading to a hidden door or wing.

The storm thundered its approval, and he heard the sound of running waters slipping eagerly downward as if the roof had a leak. He shook his head to ignore this and checked his watch. Already the storm moved off, thick rolling clouds herded across the horizon. The full moon slipped out inch by inch, and soon there wouldn't be any hope for him or the girl.

Or the people of Los Lunas.

Once the thundering subsided, the faint hints of howling —low and soft—could be heard. Tyrell's eyes fell on a battered door hidden behind a tattered curtain. He turned the knob, his ears filled with the scouring downpour of rain. Strange, because outside, no rain fell. Something about the church seemed to make everything, especially the rain, seem louder. He took in a deep breath and pushed it open to reveal...

Nina! She was tied to a chair. Her head lolled to the side, her dark brown eyes glassy and unfocused, not seeming to focus on anything. Streaks of blood raced down her face, but from what he saw, she was alive.

And not alone.

Three women, dressed in similar white robes and veils floated in the air over her, their long, wolfish tongues licking and nipping at her flesh. Their claw-like hands pawed at her wet clothes, ripping them to tatters. The dagger lay several feet from them.

Nina groaned.

The baby, nestled in her dead mother's arms, cried. Her piercing screams bounced off the room's walls. Why couldn't he hear them from outside this room? He had a feeling this space didn't sit in Los Lunas, but in some *other* place.

Scurrying to the spot, he scooped up the dagger, but the three women had already heard his entrance and descended to their feet. They howled like wild dogs, lifting their veils to reveal long snouts and bared, snarling teeth. Nina roused as soon as they left her, and she struggled, groggy against her binds.

"Run Tyrell! Run!" she shouted.

He dodged the first wolf-woman's leaping attack, but the second tackled him. They fell to the dirt-hardened floor and wrestled, her teeth snapping at his neck. He pointed his dagger at her heart. With a last hefty shove, Tyrell plunged the dagger upward into the beast's hairy body. The woman threw herself off of him, screeching and tearing at her robe.

Nina yanked and struggled against her ties, the bloodied ropes cutting more into her wrists. The third guardian whimpered as she drew herself to a standing position. The first guardian moved over to her, and they stared at Tyrell with round, gleaming eyes, their veils askew, exposing their naked, pointed teeth.

"What are those things!" Nina asked, her voice shaky and shrill.

Tyrell scooted back until he touched the wall and slid slowly up to a standing position. His eyes darted between the two remaining guardians. "Guardians. Half human, half wolf…"

Nina struggled, twisting and rotating in her chair until finally, she loosened the knots enough to wriggle her hands free and she hurried over to Tyrell. He didn't flinch. His eyes took in the deep, gash that ran across one of the guardian's robe. Blackish stains saturated the fabric, and he noticed that she had difficulty standing.

"Now what?" Nina asked, her hand outstretched for the dagger. He didn't give it to her.

"You have been bitten by them," Tyrell said, his eyes on the guardians.

They growled and lunged forward and then back, snarling.

Nina shrugged, her face sweaty. "Yeah so?"

"So," Tyrell muttered and slid away from her, inching toward the mattress on the floor where the baby had fallen silent.

From his spot, Tyrell could see it watching him, as if sizing him up with cold, calculating, *hungry* eyes that meant him harm. It watched, evaluating the fight, learning how best to defeat its enemies. Tyrell could have none of it.

It had to be destroyed.

"Nina, you have about an hour before the changes start to occur. Maybe less."

"Changes?" she said, her voice fully shaking now. She ignored it and turned to him. "Ty, what-what are you saying? What changes?"

Tyrell did not respond. Feeling his chance to act was now; he lifted the dagger and ran, full out to the mattress. The being on the flat mattress had ears, yes, they weren't human at all, but elongated, like a coyote's...yet the smooth cheeks *were* human-like a newborn...Tyrell's heart beat increased. He dropped to his knees beside the floor.

The guardians moved toward his unprotected back.

Nina searched around for a weapon, grabbed the chair, and lifted it. With a wide swing she smashed it into the slowest guardian, the one she had cut earlier. The creature howled in pain, collapsed to the floor, and whimpered like an injured dog. Ripping the leg from the chair, Nina threw it like a dagger. It smacked the second guardian's chest, but Nina had chased it, caught it mid-fall and plunged the broken end into the guardian's chest, splattering blood all over the floor, and Tyrell's back. The monster screamed, her head thrown back in immense pain.

But neither being had died. They rose up, growling, but not defeated.

On the floor, Tyrell moved the dead woman's hands and raised the dagger to just above his head. "Remus demands you to return to him!"

Without hesitation, he slammed the dagger into the creature's chest. The overhead lights flickered. As soon as the silver pierced its chest, the baby morphed, its legs extending out into hind quarters, its hands puffing out into paws. Howling in agony, the creature squirmed and thrashed about on the mattress. Clawing at the air and nipping at dust as blood gushed from its injury.

Tyrell blinked, clearing the sweat dripping into his eyes. The thing on the bed was not a baby but an alpha wolf demon, as he believed from the beginning. His faith remained intact.

The weakened guardian crawled on the floor, and the other exchanged blows with Nina. Both stopped, frozen in mid-action as if someone hit pause on the video.

The rain continued to fall, but slower, the drumming decreased to a rumble.

Out of nowhere, the guardians' bodies caught fire and burned into black ashes, right before Tyrell's eyes. The demons failed to protect the child and were no longer needed.

Bloodied and weak, Nina sunk to her knees. "Is that it? Is it over?"

Tyrell nodded, too numb to speak. Killing a wolf demon never got easier, no matter how many times he'd witnessed it. But this time *was* different. He had stuck the dagger in, not simply watched it from the sidelines. Usually, he would read the prayers that would control the guardians, and the assassin would execute the wolf.

Not this time.

The creature's howling screams eventually ceased. Only Nina's labored breathing could be heard above the rain's soft droning.

"Ty-Tyrell...please, help me..." she sputtered, her hands clawing at her throat. "Please, can't—breathe..."

"I can't help you," he whispered, the blood-drenched dagger clutched tightly in his fist. "You will change into one of them." He pointed to one of the burnt spots in the floor. "There is nothing I can do."

Nina coughed, huge chunky wads of blood splattered on to the floor. "Ty, please..."

He could hear the driving rain beat out its rhythm onto the roof like his heartbeat. What could be done? What had Cyrene nearly done when she learned that he had almost been bitten? With a quick glance downward at his right hand, he saw the silver blade, glistening under the lights in spots where drying blood didn't cover it.

"I am sorry," he said as he rapidly stepped over to her and snatched her head back by her hair. She made a feeble attempt to stop him, but her arm flapped downward without the necessary strength needed to keep it up.

Nina's teeth, clenched tight together, resembled a snarling animal. Her eyes rolled back into her head, leaving only the whites visible. Creamy foam had gathered at the corners of her lips.

Tyrell took a deep, steadying breath and whispered, "By Remus and faith that I have—I hereby release you. Be free."

He plunged the dagger point-first into the side of her slender throat with a hard-edged lump in his own. Squinting his eyes to this dreadful deed, he shoved her forward, releasing her.

Nina's blood squirted out as she fell—face forward—onto the dirt floor with a thud. Blood continued to pour into a puddle around her face.

Tears blurred his vision as he staggered out of the room, out of the church, and out into the now-drizzling mist. The moon's full face brightened the midnight partially-clouded sky.

Tyrell fell to his knees, still clutching the book, its cover dotted with reddish flecks. He held it against his chest, flat to his heart, feeling its corners dig into his sweater.

He heaved a deep breath of damp air and wept, like a heavy storm.

The End

JUSTICE

1901
New Mexico Territory

Dust crammed like a fist into Maria's throat. She choked, coughed out a thick wad of reddish stained phlegm onto the burnt orange ground. Overhead, the velvety night sky sprinkled with stars. It seemed romantic, even peaceful, but the growls of coyotes a few miles behind reminded her that no peace would be allowed this night.

"Stop! Stop!" came a hoarse bark from the gloomy dark. "¡Vuelve aquí, malvada bruja!"

It spurned not only a new rash of gooseflesh, but also a renewed jolt of fear in Maria. She stood up, wiped her blood-soaked hands across her dress and ran. Yuccas, cacti, and lizards stood idly by as she pushed her already weary and worn out body further down the dirt road. Ahead, seemingly pressed down by the evening's full moon, sat an adobe building. A place the Diné called a hogan. Its only door faced east, as the Diné required. Maria just cleared the wooden fence when the first swirls of gunfire streaked by her, lodging bullets in the building's thick red oak.

Maria didn't wait or turn. Her sandals slid on the loose dirt, the earth sliced through her tanned flesh, taking some with it. It burned and Maria bit her lip to keep from crying out aloud. The best she could do was a low, closed-lip moan. Scrambling, her breathing rough and loud in her ears, she pushed herself to a crawl, and threw herself through the partially opened door.

"Dejame en Paz!" she screamed in Spanish to the posse pursuing her. She pushed the door closed and slammed down a heavy wooden bar to keep the evil outside from rushing in to claim her. If only she'd been able do so with her heart. If only…

A huge thud shocked her away from the door. With her hands trembling, and her quivering belly trying to push its way up into her chest, Maria searched the room for anything— anything at all to protect herself. The blank walls, wooden table and chair, and blackened fire pit offered nothing—not even a cauldron for boiling or a knife for cutting—nothing at all.

Except for the weathered woman staring at her.

She was clad in the clothing of the Diné; knee-high moccasins, a desert-rose pleated skirt, a matching long-sleeve blouse and an ebony sash belt. Large oval turquoise jewelry seemed too heavy for her to wear. Hunched over as if battered by life, the wrinkled and shabby woman peered out from a thatch of silver floor-length hair. She pointed one crooked finger at Maria, moving her lined lips, nearly thin as two straps of leather, in wordless dialogue.

"I didn't mean to…" Maria shouted, tears hot and fast leaked out of her eyes. Her heart hammered so fast and loud she thought it would explode—here after all she'd been through this night. "I...forgive me."

The woman closed her eyes as if Maria's request for forgiveness offended her.

"Come out, you murderous bitch!" shouted another voice from the other side of the door. Slamming his fists against the weathered door, the man threatened to knock it from its hinges. The sheriff barked more angry words in Spanish, but Maria shut her ears to them. She'd heard them all night and she knew, with absolute certainty, that the sheriff and his posse meant only one thing—to punish her for killing Enrique.

Maria hiccupped in terror. She glanced over her shoulder to the door and then back to the elderly woman. Enrique had tried to take what he knew he should've paid for—no, no she couldn't let that action go. Her womanhood ached and had finally stopped weeping. She gulped down the acid mix of terror and adrenaline from her tongue. "I didn't mean to do..."

But she did mean to—the very second he tried to pin her to the urine-stained mattress.

"Usted lo mató. Enrique no merecía morir en sus manos falta!" yelled one of them.

One of them—the posse. A group of the sheriff's men, all carrying guns, carrying anger and fury at what she did to Enrique. Maria grimaced at that. Enrique did deserve to be punished for what he'd done to her. She hadn't expected there to be more than one of their kind, but then, she hadn't expected her actions to go unaccounted for—no, not really. What terrified her was knowing that because of Enrique's actions, she now faced the hangman's noose. She didn't mourn Enrique, or what he'd tried to take from her by force—

she fingered the violent rips in her dress, and the slivers of smeared dried blood staining the once floral patterns.

Maria felt a cold hand on her arm and she yelped.

The elderly woman's claw-like hand lay on her forearm. Dry like rusty leaves, the hand's grip tightened. With deep, liquid brown eyes, she guided Maria over to the far-right wall, closest to the fire pit.

"Don't! Please! Don't!" Maria whimpered. She couldn't hold it back. Fear forced her words out. With hands trembling, she hugged herself against the approaching gloom-filled night and the group of horsemen waiting outside. Her heart inched up into her throat. "Please, don't let them in. Don't invite them in!"

"Rest easy," the old lady comforted; her voice like broken glass, shattered Maria's panic. As she reached the front door, the Diné woman turned to look at her over the slump of her shoulder. Her eyes held a glint of knowledge, wisdom, and perhaps a deep knowing, that Maria had done something horrible, but she smiled at the frightened girl, nonetheless.

"He deserved it!" Maria muttered. "He DESERVED to die!"

The Diné woman lifted the wooden bar and threw it to the floor without so much as glance back at Maria's confession. Ripping the door open with strength Maria didn't know she had, the older woman stood against the rush of wind sweeping into the hogan for just a brief moment, before vanishing into the wind. In her place, the night swept in, screaming in intensity. With it came the sounds of hunger, rage, and revenge all twisted into one chorus.

Maria tried to fade into the wooden walls of the hogan. She couldn't speak. Her voice had dried like the desert in June. Nothing but a sharp squeak emerged. Her heart hammered fast in her chest, but no amount of pushing could take her away from here.

Away from what she'd done.

An apparition appeared in the doorway, scarlet eyes glowing in the gathering dark. From beneath the cowboy hat's brim, the sheriff's skeletal face flashed bone white from the shadows.

"Murderer..." he sang.

It raised the hair on Maria's arms. "Please, he tried to take from me, take what he was supposed to pay for!"

A stench so vile and thick hung in the air like a curtain. Maria cringed, closing her eyes to the visual horror. The low, blood curling chuckle forced her eyes open.

And what she saw chilled her heart to ice.

Just that face, the sheriff's face sneered, barely inches from her own! Where his lips should have been, were only white patches of bone. What remained of the once human face had been gleaned away, by some sharp instrument.

"Murderer..." he sang. He grabbed her neck, and with bony fingers squeezed.

"Leave me alone!" Maria pleaded between trembling lips. She lacked the strength to fight, to run, or to scream. Her terror had choked those out. She grabbed his hand, but once she touched the smooth bone, she dropped them to her side.

He didn't choke her but applied enough pressure to warn her that he could kill her. *Why? Enrique deserved to die.*

"You ain't gonna escape justice," he said.

Cold and ash pushed upward into her nostril, making her cough and gag.

"He deserved it."

The lipless mouth opened, revealing the empty blackness within.

"No one deserves to die unless Justice deems it so. You took a life. You have forsaken your own."

Icy fear thawed inside Maria. *Forsake my life? NO! Hell, no!*

At once she clawed at the skinless face, pushed against the skeletal chest, and hit the bones jutting out of the tattered shirt, but the sheriff didn't move.

Or relinquish his grasp around her neck.

"He tried to rape me," Maria coughed out. The hand tightened around her throat as if he didn't like that answer. The unyielding bone lessened a little when she spurted out, "Please!"

"You lie!" came a strangely familiar voice from the opened door. "You were paid."

"No! No!" Maria thrashed against the fixture around her neck. "No! It can't be!"

Her heart squeezed tight, wringing the blood from her face. *I stabbed him! Right through his heart! My own hands bleed and ache from the cuts I got from that damn knife slipping—so covered in your blood. I killed you! You can't be alive!*

The sheriff's hand relaxed, allowing her to look to the owner of that voice.

Her brain couldn't reconcile what she saw when he walked into the full moon's light streaming through the window. The memory of what she'd done and what she now saw didn't match up at all.

Horror inked into her body, and she screamed. It pierced the gloomy night.

Enrique stood tall—the dried and darkened blood from his fatal wound blossomed over his shirt like a flower.

"You can't-- I killed you!" Maria pushed against the hand, against the reality, against everything she'd done.

Enrique laughed—deep and hearty, full of life that Maria knew he shouldn't even possess.

He stalked toward her, his cowboy boots thick and loud on the Hogan's floor.

"You got paid for one night," Enrique's accented Spanish explained. "And you decided a little robbery would fatten your purse, while I went to get a few drinks."

"No! No, I swear!" Tears welled in Maria's eyes and spilled down her face.

"And when I got back to the room, I caught ya. While I was only going to take it outta ya in terms of pleasure, you decided it be better to get rid of me all together."

He touched the wound, the spot the knife plunged deep into.

Maria took several deep breaths in an effort to slow the beating of her heart.

The sheriff peeled her from the wall, using nothing but the unnatural strength of his hand to maneuver her.

"Release her," came the rickety voice of someone else.

The sheriff flinched, but released her. Those scarlet eyes hovered a few moments before turning into dust. Enrique behind him laughed before bursting into a gust of dirt.

Maria's lungs forced her to take deep breaths. From behind her, a cold breeze rustled against her flesh, raising goose flesh. Another presence was in the small eight-sided space; Maria turned slowly. Perhaps it was the old woman returning. Relief washed over Maria. The older woman was safe.

"A dream," Maria said to herself. "Yes, only a dream."

She swallowed and wiped her tear-stained face. Maria huffed out the remnants of her fear and tried to put the awful event behind her. Enrique had had it coming. For months, he'd visit the brothel, pay a pathetic price for her time, and then proceed to use her in every manner he saw fit. Yes, at first she enjoyed it, fell in love with him and looked forward to his arrival. But when she'd asked him to marry her tonight, to take her away from this horrid place, he'd laughed. Laughed! She made him pay for the violation of her hope. Nothing short of his death would do to ease the sharp stab of loss in her heart. She'd thank the elder woman and leave. If she started now, she might make it as far as the Rio Grande before tomorrow evening.

Turning to face the elderly woman, Maria said, "Gracias."

But the warmth vanished as she met the elder woman's eyes. Maria recoiled in horror, tumbling to the floor.

The old Diné woman pointed at her and with eyes full of knowing said, "No one escapes justice, especially those who harm my grandson."

"Grandson?' Maria inquired. How did the elderly woman know Enrique? Why, why would she call him grandson? None of it made any sense.

Before Maria could make sense of it, the elderly woman bent down, snatched up a pile of dirt—that had once been the sheriff and lifted her claw-like fist with purpose.

"Si," the elderly woman spat. "My son fell in love and married Enrique's mother. At first, I did not approve, but Enrique was a beautiful boy. A good man. One who helped his Diné people as well as his Mexican family. One you killed. You will not escape justice."

The elderly woman blew the New Mexican dirt from her opened palm, directly into Maria face. Maria shrieked as her flesh melted off her skeleton. Burning so fierce, so wretched, all she could do was scream.

Those screams echoed for hours, until the last of the light from the moon outside disappeared into the horizon.

The End

KQ'

(PRONOUNCED "KOH")

A tickling softness brushed Yazhi's fingertips as her mother's blanket slid out of her hands. Her mother folded it in a quick fashion before picking up another one. The frenzied actions were being repeated all over the village. An ochre glow rimmed the village. The entire land seemed to have captured the sun in its mouth and burped up flames. As the fire crawled across the mesa, it chewed up everything in its path. Bold and brave, it fought back the cold darkness. The forces jumped onto the edge of their lands and crept ever closer.

The smoke rose into the sky and thickened with each passing moment. Wails, hurried voices, and the sharp tones of the villagers echoed on the ash-thick air. They had to push on, for Black God had erupted here, in this place—their place. It meant nothing for him to escape the confines of their hogan, and began to ravage the land, turning the tumbleweeds, cacti, and man into its food. Terror shook Yazhi, for she'd never seen anything like this before.

This was her first contact with Black God. The son of a

comet and fire, Black God was lord of kq', fire. Tales told by her grandfather, a powerful medicine man, spoke of Black God's cowardice and transformative powers.

How could they believe Black God was helpless when he chewed the landscape and ravished all in his path? With eyes wide, Yazhi clutched her mother's dress with mounting fear. The soft fur of her mother's blanket offered small comfort. It hung from her shoulders as she bent down to retrieve a fallen basket.

Yazhi shut her eyes and turned her face into the fur.

"What ails her?" her father demanded, his voice rough from the smoke.

"Black God's power is displayed this night. It is Yazhi's first time in his presence." Her mother coughed. "It comes closer."

Her father growled. When Yazhi looked at him, she saw him shake his head in mounting disappointment, but whether that was for the situation or her actions, she didn't know.

"Here. Take these."

Her mother gave Yazhi a small smile, and pressed items into her hands. Bits of pottery filled with grain, oil, and turquoise. She followed her mother's glance to the semi-circle of fire, kq', that leapt up and vanished into the billowing sky. At the same time, kq' managed to remain on the ground. As if angered, it crackled and popped in its efforts to speak to them, even as it consumed all in its path. Her people had to leave before they too became food for the kq's belly.

She had never before seen it so wild and untamed.

Yazhi spoke soft against the thick air. "What do you want?"

The maize lay collected in hand-woven baskets, ready for the journey to the neighboring village. As the elders told of the first people, First Woman and First Man were joined forever by this world to those that had come before them. The different types of maize represented the various people who eventually became the Diné. The flickering called to Yazhi to come, to touch, and to feel its power.

Entranced, she headed toward it.

Black God's kq'. It moved across the mesa, old and slow like the god himself, but then fast and furious. She pictured herself standing tall in its orange-yellow glow as First Woman once did in the yellow world, when she first met Black God.

Like Yazhi tonight.

Somehow she'd walked closer to the kq' than to her home. Mesmerized, she watched it dance for her and she reached out her hand to join in its joy. Now that she had come closer, it did not seem so bad.

"Ow!" She yelped as flames bit her. She rubbed the angry spot on her hand.

Her mother stuck her head out of the hogan's entrance. "Yazhi?"

Yazhi waved. "Here!"

Her mother's face became alarmed. "Yazhi! Get away from that fire!"

"But...."

"Now! Come closer to me, beside the house." She waited until Yazhi had started back toward the hogan, but the clatter and clang from inside the dwelling drew her attention away.

All around the family hogan, people trekked back and forth between their homes, mules, and horses. Yazhi's mother continued to bring out items and tie them onto the family's own pack animals.

Once her mother had disappeared back into the hogan, Yazhi turned back to the fire. She couldn't take her eyes away from its newfound display of magic. The growing kq' battled back the gloom, a fierce and greedy warrior. She found herself back at the edge of the blaze, within arm's reach once more.

Moving closer to her village, the kq' gobbled everything in its path. Its power grew as it fed. When it appeared to be winning the eternal fight, it reached higher to the dark sky as if summoning its lord.

Yazhi stumbled backward. Her items spilled to the earth. The heat licked at her as if finding her delicious. She searched behind for her mother or someone, but there was only the constant motion of people on the move.

These weren't the only movements in the night.

Yazhi watched as the moon overhead folded in to the gathering dark, and stepped down onto the ground in front of her. Obediently the fire withdrew, but only from the place of darkness, where he stood. It was Black God! She couldn't mistake him. His mouth was a full moon, and a crescent moon had been etched into his forehead. Elderly and mysterious, his smile frightened her.

The kq' leapt around excitedly, like children did when their parents came home.

"Come into my embrace, little one," Black God encouraged.

"Why?" Yazhi wanted to run, but she couldn't get her feet to obey. Her mouth struggled to form words. The fact that she'd managed to ask the one question surprised her.

"Because I demand it." He did not smile now. His face was hidden in shadow. Coward.

The whims of gods were legendary. Yazhi looked around, but no one else seemed to notice Black God towering into the heavens. She swallowed her fear and tried to look up into his face. Where did he want to take her? She didn't want to leave her family. It had been his doing that her people had to leave this settlement. Yazhi knew her family, like other Diné', had grown tired of being uprooted, first by the white men, and now this.

So, she steeled her strength and pooled her courage. First Woman did not shy away from this lazy god, who let his offspring do his work for him. Neither would she. He could demand whatever he wanted, but she had some demands of her own.

"No." Yazhi tossed her plaits over her shoulder. With her hands on her narrow hips she glared at him, but only a moment before looking away.

"No?" He rumbled when he spoke and the sky shook.

For a god of kq', he made her very cold.

Someone cried out and she looked across to the many people streaming across the horizon. Sheep, mules, and people displaced by Black God's appetite—or whim.

Yazhi turned back to Black God. "I will come with you, but you must stop destroying the village."

"I will destroy this valley, the mesa, and your village and you will come with me." He waved his hand and the raging ochre grew higher.

"I am the granddaughter of Chief Manuelito! You will not threaten me or my people!"

She stamped her foot. Inside, a magic warmth spread through her, filling her with light that poured from her fingertips. Her heart thundered in her chest as she directed them into the eyes of Black God, who screamed in agony.

He could burn her to ash where she stood! That knowledge terrified her. But all the pent- up disappointment, rage, and confidence of youth ignited her own inner kq'.

Besides, Yazhi reasoned, Black God had already devoured much of the land surrounding her village, if not the homes themselves.

"Yazhi?" Her mother poked her head out of the hogan's

doorway. Her dark hair blew on the breeze, but it failed to hide the fear on her face. "Come!"

When Yazhi turned back to look at Black God, he had vanished. His chuckling echoed on the wind. The moon hung in its full glory in the heavens above, and all appeared as it had been before.

Yazhi checked her hands. They seemed ordinary. No light. No scars. Nothing.

"We are leaving!" her father called as he climbed on the horse. He waved his family to him, and Yazhi raced to join them. He sounded tired, but strength showed in his movements. He would endure. Their people would endure, as they have forever, for the Diné.

The air tasted like ash, smoke, and dirt. Yazhi too smelled of smoke, and her moccasins were covered in soot. She glanced once more at the village, then back to the kq'. She'd done what she could to save her village, but the flames continued to advance.

Her efforts had been in vain.

"Look! The fires are changing!" Her mother pointed to the orange glow that winked out near the first set of hogans. It looked as if stronger kq' had taken hold on the western edge of the lands, closer to the canyons—away from their village.

Black God was turning his glowing offspring. Like a starving sheep, the kq' demonstrated its powerful appetite, consuming everything in its path. But as it continued its dance with the wind, it moved away from the village.

Her mother hugged Yazhi to her as her father joined them. They watched the darkness and the illumination of the kq' engaged in battle.

Yazhi rested her head on her mother's shoulder. "Do we still have to leave?"

"No, little one. We do not." Her mother kissed her forehead. "We do have to bring everything back into our home."

Yazhi groaned, and both her parents laughed.

"Watch the kq', Yazhi, as it continues its dance with its partner, the wind," her mother encouraged.

Yazhi looked out to the destroyed lands. She'd never seen anything so beautiful, and so harsh before.

She hoped she never would again.

The End

UNHINGED: A TALE OF THREE BROTHERS

"How did it happen?" Julio asked, his tone tight and hard, like the land all around Wild Sage County.

"Gun shot." Herman grunted and spat a gooey wad of tobacco onto the cracked pavement. He'd answered so fast, the words bled together, as if to linger on the topic would make him remember the bloody mess of brains and bone that used to be Carlos. *It's too much.* He squeezed his hazel eyes shut to wash out the vision. God the mess! The smell! The blood. So. Much. Blood.

As the brother of Carlos Estrada, Herman, only ten minutes prior to Julio's arrival at the morgue, identified what remained of his sibling. As eldest, it had to be him to give official identification. Still, Julio looked much older than his droopy eyes, round beer-belly and sagging shoulders conveyed. He seemed to be in his late fifties, not his mid-thirties.

The metallic taste from the morgue mixed with the rotting odors of death, bleach, and bile. When Herman opened his eyes, he breathed a sigh of relief that the vision of his dead brother had disappeared. But the odor remained lodged in his nostrils—a sickening reminder of a life sliced short.

"They have any idea who shot him?" Julio squinted against the bright New Mexican sun. "Damn, it's bright out here."

"No." Herman felt like crying. His whole being threatened to shatter into a million drops of anguish. Carlos was dead. Dead!

With a sigh, Herman massaged his tired face. "Yeah." The overall sadness seemed to slip out from the police station like a hand, clawing its way out of the earth and scratching against his clothes.

With a county line of only thirty miles, it didn't take anyone long to drive from point A to point B in Cubero, New Mexico. The Cubero Police included three folks. Old lady Gerry answered the dispatch, but it had been Sheriff Travis who called Herman that afternoon. They'd found Carlos, but not among the living.

The wind blew hard, wrapping Julio's jacket tight around him, and whipping his long, black ponytail about his neck. He didn't flinch. Herman doubted if Julio felt the biting coldness of the approaching night, because right at that moment, he, himself, felt numb.

Julio stood on the steps of the police station. He stared at the closed white doors for several minutes, before starting for the vehicle. *He really looks old.*

Herman got in the truck and slumped down in the passenger seat. "Can we go now? I need to get out of here."

Julio walked down the sidewalk and opened the truck's driver side door. Just like dad. They did not speak as Julio started the truck, flipped on the heat, and backed out of the parking spot. He yanked down the sun visor and slipped on his sunglasses. "Damn it."

As Herman watched the police station grow smaller in the passenger side mirror with an ache burning in his throat, forcing it to close as he fought to swallow. Grief felt like he'd swallowed fire. He choked it down, but it felt like golf ball-sized stones. It tasted bitter, like ashes, and he hated himself. The swallowing did not help, for soon tears leaked out from his half-closed eyes and hurried down his thin cheeks. Carlos had vanished, and he had been powerless to stop it.

"You cryin'?" Julio barked with a short angry glance at Herman.

Herman couldn't respond. How could he? His throat burned with tears. No answer he could give Julio would be right anyway.

"Carlos was a punk! A soon-to-be convict..." Julio shouted as he burrowed down the street. "He wasn't all he seemed on the outside, Herm. He was a monster, I tell you."

"Don't!" Herman lashed back, causing Julio to swerve into the on-coming lane. "Don't talk about him like-like he's some animal or some weirdo! He wasn't a monster. He was my brother!"

Julio fell into a shocked silence. His eyes remained focused on the road, and his lips pressed into a tight, thin line. The muscle in his jaw throbbed to a rhythm all its own.

Herman's heart beat raced, and he placed his hand over his chest to stop it from escaping. What had just gotten into him? He'd never spoken to Julio like that before—ever. He snatched away from him and turned his attention to the landscape smearing outside his window.

When their father died, Julio dropped out of school to take care of them, him being the oldest. Mami relied on him. Heck, they all did. Julio raised him, for Pete's sake. He raised Carlos too. Talking back to him like that, even shouting at Julio—unthinkable. Disrespectful.

He had always obeyed and respected Julio—always.

Now, Carlos, on the other hand, was Momma's baby boy. He and Julio argued constantly and when Carlos turned eighteen, Julio turned him out of the house on his ear. Herman still lived at home, but he didn't fight or balk at Julio's orders of the house. He toed the line, because Julio could get, well, angry. So Herman kept his head down and lived his life beneath his eldest brother's gaze.

Herman could still hear the screaming between his two brothers that day Carlos left for good.

"Get goin', demon!" Julio roared, the wad of tobacco pressing against his inside cheek like a tumor. "Before I put you out of your misery!"

"This is Mami's house and if she want me gone, then I'll leave!" Carlos screamed back. His muddy-brown eyes seemed to glow in the afternoon sun. "It don't matter if you like it, I do!"

Julio's eyes widened in fury and he jerked Carlos up to his tiptoes by the throat. His large, wide hands closed like a slow-moving vice against Carlos's warm copper skin. "Evil has no place in this house! Ya hear?"

He shoved Carlos hard. So hard in fact, he stumbled backward and fell off the porch, down the steps, and into the New Mexican dirt and thick mud.

Rapid and furious Spanish followed.

Three nights passed without Carlos. Mami pitched a fit and he moved right back in after the brief hiatus. Julio always said that Carlos held some sort of magic over her. Some sort of spell that made her turn into mush and give him whatever he wanted. Witchcraft, Julio used to say, the devil's spawn.

"You still alive over there?" Julio's rough voice sounded hard and cut into Herman's memory.

Herman nodded, "Yeah."

They cruised down Ortega Avenue. Julio stopped at the stop sign at the intersection, leaned out his window, and spat out the lowered window. Herman heard the splat as it hit the pavement and cringed. On they went. Past Old Gregory's Liquor, Rhonda's Roasted Peppers, and Cellia's Ceramics and Cards—used to be Cellia's Mexican Cooking only three years ago. More tourist hot spot than any other place in town, the downtown area, had 12 shops.

About a mile from their home, Julio spoke again. "I just don't want you wastin' your tears, Her. He was odd, weird, and vile. And the company he kept..."

Herman nodded, but said nothing. He felt drained as if someone removed his emotional cork and his feelings poured out of him, spilling all over the floor of the truck.

———

Herman awoke to a pitch-black room and a chill seeping through the window. As he rubbed sleep from his eyes, and clear his mental cobwebs, the roaring of laughter drifted in from the living room television. His neck ached, and he realized he had been asleep for only a few hours. Rolling his neck to try to loosen the muscles, he sat up, and peered about the darkened room.

None of the objects looked familiar to him in the gloomy shadows. In his dresser's spot sat what looked to be a clothes hamper. Beneath the window, a bookshelf crammed with shoes, not his usual clothes-covered desk. With mounting horror, he realized that this wasn't his room.

It was Carlos's!

He threw off the covers, leapt from the bed and hurried out of the room, gasping for air at the horrifying thought that he had slept in his dead brother's bed.

Coughing and holding his stomach, he burst into the living room.

Julio looked up from the television. "What's the matter with you?"

Herman struggled to stand, but the pinch in his side kept him bent over. With his hands on his knees, he swallowed, tried to convey in words his terror, but gave up to only shaking his head.

Everything is wrong.

Julio turned his attention back to the basketball game. As Herman approached the couch, he could see a large glass filled with beer on one side of Julio's feet and a yellow plastic bowl filled with popcorn in his lap.

"You missed the first quarter. UNM is getting stomped." Julio shook his head in disappointment.

He'd changed shirts, but otherwise he looked the same as earlier. Julio took a fistful of popcorn and stuffed it into his mouth. Before he could swallow, he lifted the beer to his mouth and gulped. For the first time in a while, Julio looked relieved—almost happy. The new growth that usually occupied the lower parts of his face had been shaved. Herman scowled in disbelief. Julio almost looked clean and groomed.

What. The. Hell?

Too abashed and confounded to move, Herman remained rooted to the spot. Sure, it was Thursday night. And yeah, on Thursdays, Julio saddled up with a beer and popcorn to watch whatever sport was on, but this was ridiculous. Carlos had been shot today.

Shot *dead*.

Didn't Julio care about the death of their brother? Not that Julio was a warm and fuzzy guy. He wasn't. But this lack of emotion or any sort of feeling beside apathy was *unsettling*.

"You know, Carlos died today. Shouldn't we be planning the funeral and contacting his friends and mom's family in Albuquerque?"

Julio glanced up at Herman, palmed popcorn suspended in mid-air. "Yeah. Damn shame, but I feel safer knowing he ain't around no more."

Herman couldn't speak. He pointed to the popcorn and the television as if he was suddenly struck mute.

Julio's small eyes followed Herman's pointing. With a shrug, he turned back to the screen. "Sure. It's a game night. I haven't felt this wonderful in years, Herm."

The gut punch caused Herman to stumble. Okay. Julio handled most emotional things differently, and this could be how he dealt with death. Who's to say it was weird? Didn't he just sleep in his brother's bed? Deciding to stop overreacting and deal with his own grief, Herman headed to the kitchen for dinner.

Their mother passed away a few years ago, and since that time he did most of the cooking in the house. But, Julio had decided on eating popcorn, so Herman fixed himself a sandwich and returned to his bedroom, making sure to enter the third door on the left, not the second.

He closed the door quietly behind him and surveyed the room to make sure that it was indeed his. He sat down on his full-size bed, a bed he had since his youth, and swallowed bites of his sandwich. A sense of being out of his body hit him like a truck. Almost as if he stood at the door's threshold witnessing a being that looked like him ate his bologna and cheese sandwich with all the interest of a robot observer. When he was done, he lay back onto the bed and stared up at the ceiling.

Torn between his grief over Carlos and his dismay at Julio's behavior, Herman didn't know whether to cry or rage. Julio had called him a monster. Carlos had done strange things, like howl at full moons in the middle of the night; disappear for days without telling anyone, only to return home with strange tattoos and dark, heavy circles under his eyes. But Carlos was a wild teenager—young and free.

Everyone knew how strange and weird teenagers could be.

Besides, that had been years ago, long before Mami died, and the world moved on.

———

Several hard knocks against the door forced Herman awake. He rubbed his eyes against the daylight pouring in its brightness. Groaning, he realized, he'd slept in his clothes. With his muscles aching, he got out of bed slowly. The knocks on the door increased in volume and urgency, forcing him to hurry.

Outside, on the porch, Travis Martin, a local police officer, launched into another round of police-knocks. Herman and Travis had attended high school together, like most of the people in Cubero.

Travis had wanted to be a Marine but failed basic training due to an enormous ego that wouldn't be flattened by shouts, push-ups, or drills ordered by the drill sergeant. They shipped him right back to the town with his pride smarting and his anger issues turned to full-blast.

"Morning, Travis." Herman tried to make his still sleepy tongue work.

Travis smiled, fleshing out his sole dimple. That dimple made him the most popular guy in school, and even now, melted most women's hearts down at the Three-Sixty bar.

"Just looking for your brother." He tried to look over Herman's shoulders.

Herman frowned. He didn't know what time it was, but he could tell it was early enough for Travis to know that Julio would be at work.

"Well, he ain't here." Herman grumbled, now fully awake.

Travis shrugged making his muscular shoulders flex against his uniform.

"He ain't at work neither."

Herman stepped out onto the porch in his rumpled clothes. "What's this about? Did you find out something about who shot Carlos? Tell me and I'll pass it on to Julio."

Travis smiled again, but this time it wasn't handsome, but cold—sinister. "Now, Herm, this is official police business. Just tell Julio to get down to the station when he comes home tonight."

With that he turned and headed back to his cruiser. The vehicle shot out of their driveway and into the residential road with fury.

Herman remained on the porch as he watched Travis drive away, kicking up gravel as he drove off into the New Mexican dawn. Herman wondered where Julio had gone. His eldest brother never missed work except for their parents' funerals and that one time he accidentally shot himself in the foot.

Herman went back into the house and called Julio's job in Grants. As he waited for the receptionist to pick up, he wondered why Travis came out to the house. He could have called to see if Julio was home, or to discuss whatever "police business" he wanted.

"Ed Corley Ford. Get the car you deserve. This is Margaret. How may I help you?" Margaret sounded as cheery and bright as a new day.

Herman winced.

"Margaret, it's Herman. Is Julio around?" He felt foolish asking if his brother was at work. His brother was *always* at work.

"Hmmm...Herman, Julio took bereavement today," Margaret said lazily.

The image of Travis's crestfallen face melted as Herman tried to turn his attention back to what Margaret was talking about.

"What?" He didn't hear her right. "Please repeat that, Marge."

"I said, *suga*, that your brother ain't here today. I gotta go, hon, my phone is lighting up like the fourth of July."

Herman hung up. Stunned and more than a little confused, he placed the receiver back into the cradle and left the kitchen. He crept up the steps to check if Julio was in his room. Their brother had been killed yesterday. He could've slept in. Herman had just assumed he'd gone into work.

Grief often came in many forms, none of them right or wrong. Julio had been acting strange since the news of Carlos's murder. Perhaps a little time alone would help him grieve, Herman thought as he reached the top of the landing. He made a right into the room designated as Julio's. Through the cracked door, he could see the *Alien* posters and the newspaper clippings about the Roswell landing. Magazines about aliens covered parts of the floor. The bed was made up and nothing seemed amiss.

"Julio, you in here?" Herman called.

He glanced across the hallway to the bathroom, and noted that it too was clean, orderly and … vacant.

Julio was gone.

Panic rose in his throat, but he fought against it. Maybe Julio went fishing or hunting to be alone. Herman coughed out a sigh and took a deep breath. He had to get a hold of himself. Carlos's funeral arrangements had to be done.

Herman entered the room, thinking that perhaps there might be a note left for him or some explanation as to where his brother had gone. The somewhat tidy room had nothing out of place, except for the mess of magazines on the floor, and in fact, the bed didn't even look slept in.

A breeze from an open window blew its cool, morning air across Herman's face.

"Maybe the note blew off and under the bed." He dropped to the floor and lifted the bed skirt.

Underneath the bed hid a cluster of clothing items and they reeked of stale sweat. Sighing at the carelessness, Herman grabbed the bundled of clothes and pulled them from beneath the bed. Julio knew better than to leave dirty clothes under the bed. A perfectly empty clothes hamper sat less than a foot from the bed. In fact, Herman was surprised to find them. Julio was usually a neat-freak.

As the clothes came from darkness and into the light, Herman recognized the tee-shirt Julio wore yesterday. He could make out dark patches, a spray of some sort around the front side of the shirt. It smelled horrible and he held his breath as he leaned in closer.

Yesterday, he thought it was mud from outside or oil grease from his job.

In the illumination of a new day, it resembled dried blood.

Herman dropped the shirt and stuffed it back under the

bed where he had found it. With trembling hands, he left the room.

What did Julio do that involved so much blood? Hunting and fishing involved blood, but not working at the service department at Corley's Ford. Julio didn't have any injuries Herman could see.

Unsettled, Herman crept out of Julio's bedroom and back down the stairs.

———

J ulio came home around five o'clock, his usual time. Herman waited in the living room. With the television off, he hoped to talk to his brother, man to man. He wanted some answers and had spent the better part of the day making funeral arrangements for Carlos. It didn't bother him to help his brother's final resting place be one that represented the life he lived. He *didn't* like contacting their family and Carlos's friends to notify them of the loss. That hurt, and it drained him emotionally. He'd cried a lot.

"Hola, there you are!" Julio came in, sat down, and took off his boots. "Whew! What a day! Everybody wanted their car washed. Mud everywhere after that hard rain the other day."

Herman raised his eyebrows but said nothing.

Julio wiped his face with his hands. "What did you do all day? Study for that chemistry exam?"

"No. I made funeral arrangements for Carlos." Even to him, his voice sounded flat, defeated. He hadn't even gotten to the good point of the conversation yet.

"You did what?" Julio's lopsided grin faltered.

"I made Carlos's funeral arrangements. The service is Sunday."

"Why are you paying good money to bury him? Let the town take care of it."

A chill had crossed Herman's back.

Catching his look, Julio added, "I mean, I loved him, but he's dead. Let's move on with our lives. You've been waddling around here all day and slept all yesterday afternoon."

Anger rose again in Herman's throat, and his cheek grew hot with fury. He steadied his voice before speaking. "The town will dump him in a pauper's lot, without a headstone or marker. He deserves better than that."

"Look, Herm..."

"He was a good man! Sure, his friends were odd, but Carlos was good."

Julio stood up and crossed the small distance between his recliner and the couch, where Herman sat. "Don't you go lying! He was a good for nothing. A, a--"

"A what?" Herman whispered, holding his brother's rage-filled gaze.

"A freakin' alien! People ain't what they seem, Herm! Wake up!"

Herman cowered back. Julio's flushed face held bulging eyes and the vein across his forehead throbbed. His hands curled into tight fists.

He'd never acted like this. What the hell was the matter with him?

"Travis came by here looking for you today," Herman stuttered out. A mixture of anger and pride had uncoiled and threatened to engulf him.

Stunned, Julio ran his fingers through his thinning hair as he fell back from Herman. "Travis? For what?"

Herman shrugged. "He was looking for you."

Julio wiped his mouth and the color drained from his face.

Instead of the violent, angry purplish-red of moments before, his face had become ashen beneath his skin.

"For me? What did he say?" Julio asked, wiping his mouth with the back of his arm.

Herman wondered if there was an echo in the room. "What's going on? I don't like this."

Julio backed away from the couch as if Herman had a disease. He plopped down in the recliner and looked across to him, with what looked like unseeing, glassy eyes. His mouth opened and closed like a fish out of water.

"Julio, are you all right?" Herman struggled to push down his annoyance.

He nodded. "Fine. Fine."

"He said you weren't at work today," Herman said.

"I-I was there." Julio stared up at the ceiling.

"No, I called. Marge said you took bereavement."

Julio wiped his face again and closed his eyes.

Herman waited and the tension in the room thickened. "Where were you?"

"You don't need to know that." Julio answered.

"But...Travis was looking for you and..."

"So what!" Julio roared. "They ain't got nothin' on me! Nothin'!"

"What?" Herman stopped himself when he saw Julio's face twist with mounting rage.

"And you," he barked, his pointed finger directed at Herman's chest, "stay out of my freakin' business!"

With that, he snatched up his boots and climbed the steps to his room, pounding each step with bloody fury. His bedroom door slammed hard against its frame and rattled the house.

But Julio's comments rattled Herman even more. What did he mean the police didn't have anything on him? Why was he telling him to stay out of his business? Something was going on with him, and it frightened Herman to think of what.

He went to the kitchen and fixed a pot of coffee. The kitchen's sole light source illuminated the small, worn place. Despite its age, Herman recalled many happy memories, of his mother making birthday cakes, of his aunt and uncle from Las Cruces who came for Thanksgiving, and of his dad using the gas stove eye to light his cigarettes. This once was a place of love, respect, and familia.

He remembered the time Carlos got his hand caught in the freezer door handle. Julio, who was taller, didn't want to get his ice cream, so a determined, but smaller Carlos tried to get it himself. He fell from the chair and got his wrist caught in the door handle's small opening. Julio laughed when Carlos cried. Julio watched Carlos squirm and twist as he tried to free his wrist, his legs dangled in the air. His wrist broken.

Julio said he wanted to see if Carlos was truly human. In the end, the awful experiment revealed only pain and suffering. Carlos broke his wrist and wore a cast for months. Momma had been outraged, grounding Herman and Julio because neither helped Carlos. Never mind that Herman had run to get her.

The feud between the oldest and the youngest dragged on. Julio used to always call Carlos a freak, a weirdo, an alien, and it used to burn Carlos to an angry red.

Herman didn't really feel left out. Momma called him "the peacemaker." He often tried to make situations civil between them—being the one in the middle. After each blow up, Herman came up with the solutions and the compromises.

Carlos wasn't perfect, and a kernel of truth resided in Julio's claims of Carlos's friends' characters, but his brother didn't deserve to die.

He had to know what Travis knew about Carlos's death and what he knew about Julio.

———

"I told you, Herm. It's police business." Travis smiled at him and exposed his white, even teeth. Something about it reminded Herman of alligators. Big, wide, and deadly.

He suppressed a shudder. Drawing himself to his full height, he stepped closer to Travis. "It's my brother."

"It's confidential," Travis said with a shake of his head. He spread his hands out as if to say it was out of his hands.

"We went to school together. All twelve years. You know me. This is my family, Travis."

Travis sighed. He looked out of his office window, got up from his desk, and shut the door. He came around to sit back down. He put his hat on the desk and sighed.

"Okay, but you're not going to like it." Travis let the bravado slip. "If you repeat this, I will deny we ever had this conversation. You hear me?"

"Yeah. Just tell me," Herman said.

Travis reached into his desk and took out an 8½-by-11 inch manila folder. He took his time to open it, making sure to turn all crime scene photos over so that Herman couldn't see them. He flipped the pages until he reached the report.

"You ready to hear this?" Travis asked, eyebrows arched in doubt.

Butterflies danced around in Herman's stomach. He took in a deep breath, held it, and then let it out real slow. "Yeah. I'm ready."

"We have reason to believe that Julio shot Carlos." Travis held up the forensics report. "When he came yesterday, we asked him some questions, clipped his fingernails, and did the gun residue test on his hands. We asked him a few questions too. Julio had gun residue on his hands."

A buzzing filled Herman's ears and he suddenly felt sick to his stomach. No wonder it felt like Julio had been in there for hours. Still in shock, he couldn't tell if it was his imagination or reality.

"What?" He hadn't heard Travis right.

"We suspect that your brother, Julio, shot and killed, your *other* brother, Carlos, two days ago. It happened up in the desert arroyo outside the east part of the town." Travis answered, but his brown eyes seemed sad. "We found your brother's fingerprints on the shell casing we recovered up there, too."

"Oh, no. That's can't be right. He was at work that day. I called him when you guys found Carlos," Herman sounded calm, but his world had begun to tilt.

"Carlos had only been dead for 4 to 6 hours. That would put both of your brothers together sometime that morning." Travis started putting the items back into the envelope.

"No, Julio was at work." Herman couldn't think of anything else to say. None of it made sense.

Now it was Travis's turn to shake his head. "I checked his timesheet. Julio came in late that day. He didn't get there until 11:30."

"11:30," Herman repeated.

Travis nodded. "Herm, look, I know it's hard. But try to remember. Does Julio own a shotgun?"

"Yes, but so do a lot of people 'round here." He didn't have to think about it because Julio owned several shotguns. So did just about everyone in town.

"We believe Julio picked up Carlos that morning, probably after you left the house for school. Took him up there and shot him," Travis explained in a voice filled with pity.

"For what reason? They were brothers!" Once again, the burning springs started in his eyes. Already rimmed raw from Carlos, Herman's eyes struggled to water despite their strong urge to do so.

Travis only nodded. "They didn't like each other. Everyone in town knew that."

"So, they argued sometimes. They were brothers and deep down they loved each other!" Tears formed in the corners of his eyes. He didn't want to cry in front of Travis. His throat burned, and he felt hot all over.

"You're wrong." Travis sat motionless in his chair, staring at Herman with what could only be described as an ever-increasing amount of pity.

Herman closed his eyes and tried his best to maintain his composure. What evidence did they have? A fingerprint on a shell casing? Nothing a good lawyer couldn't explain away. Maybe Julio went up there to just shoot his gun. That would explain the casings.

Travis sighed. "There is one more thing, well, two more things. We found your brother's DNA under Carlos's fingernails. We also found Julio's girlfriend from Grants who said that lately he'd been telling her that Carlos wasn't human. That he was an alien, like some damn T.V. show."

"Julio didn't really believe in aliens, and first contact and stuff. That's just what he teased Carlos about. I mean, that goes back years." Herman frowned, the budding of relief in his body. *They don't have anything to prove Julio did this.*

"It would seem that Julio told her that Carlos was an alien or, it says here a *creature*." Travis's eyebrows rose in doubt. "Seems he needs to be locked away in a nuthouse— no offense, Herm. We think he might have shot Carlos as a way to rid himself of the," Travis cleared his throat, "creature."

Travis fell silent, shrugged his shoulders, and kept his gaze on Herman.

"Julio ain't crazy. You've got to believe me...he ain't off." Herman shot out of the seat and started pacing the floor.

Travis leaned across his desk and patted Herman's hand. "We're coming for him today, Herm. Get him a good lawyer —maybe one of the fancy ones from Santa Fe."

Herman drew back and hugged himself. With a fast glance up at Travis, he said, "Thanks for the warning."

Travis stood up too. "Don't do anything stupid."

Herman didn't answer but left the police station. His chest felt tight and his breath escaped in sips. The thunderous dark sky threatened snow, but he paid it no attention.

A storm already raged deep within him.

———

A short time later, as he reached his house's well-worn steps, Herman pulled back the screen and pushed open the door. No one locked their doors in Cubero.

"Stop right there!" Julio's voice, high and strained, screamed at him. "I see ya!"

Herman's eyes adjusted to the dusky interior. Why were the lights off? He peered around the room until his eyes landed on Julio. The shotgun was aimed at Herman. From the shadows, Julio's wild eyes showed a lot of white.

"Julio, what the heck are you doin'?" Fear seized Herman's throat and threatened to crush his windpipe. Travis's words floated back to haunt him. *Seems he needs to be locked away in a nuthouse...*

"I know you're one of them..." Julio hissed. "I can smell you—you green-blood alien!"

"What? I'm your brother!" Herman stepped toward him.

"That other one said that too! Just before I blew it to bits!" Julio waved his gun up and down before steadying it.

"That's a load of hogwash! Come on. If I'm alien, so are you!" Herman tried to stop the trembling that seized him. "Put it down! Stop this craziness!"

Reason. Listen to reason. Surely it would sink into that thick skull. Beads of sweat slipped down Herman's face. He could see Julio hands put the shotgun down.

With a sigh of relief, Herman stepped closer to him, happy for the entire affair to be over. He'd take Julio down to Albuquerque and get him some help. If he acted quickly, they could get packed and gone before Travis arrived to question or arrest him.

A silver flash appeared in Julio's hand.

For a moment, for it could hardly be longer, Herman's mind transmitted the question, but it failed to come out of his mouth. *What the heck?*

By the time he recognized the handgun in the gloomy kitchen, it was too late.

Julio shouted, "I'll be damned if I live life as an alien!"

A click and a bang followed.

Then silence.

The blood splattered across Herman's face and torso. The warm liquid dripped down his face like heart-wrenching tears.

The End

THE TRADER

The thunderous rain nearly drowned out the doorbell's ring as Joe Yazzie walked into the pawn shop. The trader, James Tanner, hurried from the rear stock room with an expression of calm, comfortable greed that faded the moment he saw his sole customer.

"Ya-ta-hey," James muttered from beneath his dirt-brown moustache; his hazel eyes traveled over Joe's dusty jeans and weathered face. An expression of dislike replaced his calm demeanor, and he carefully sniffed the air—alcohol and vagrancy went hand-in-hand here in the heart of Indian country. The natives did little more than drink their reparation checks and beg for money. No, he wasn't in the mood to deal with that today. He had the local police on speed dial.

Joe nodded but did not meet James's eyes. At best it seemed Joe could barely lift his eyes above the enclosed glass cases of Navajo pottery, Zuni silversmiths' jewelry, and Acoma bowls. His ragged clothes and filthy hands didn't try to touch the display case, for which James was glad.

He had just cleaned that case.

James let out a slow breath of air and said, "What can I do for ya?"

The Navajo man reached into his worn sack and with grime-encrusted hands, removed a humble, old piece of pottery. The bowl, no taller than a can of soda and slightly warped, looked even shabbier under the overhead fluorescent lights of the pawn shop. The pot's lip was chipped, and around its body were crudely carved lumps of clay which seemed to resemble faces, twisted and contorted into painful, even tortured expressions. James grimaced beneath his bushy moustache, his upper lip buried in the bristles.

"This is it?" James said with a smirk, hardly hiding his contempt for the piece. *Why do these people continue to come here with shit?*

Joe shuffled and mumbled something that sounded like Navajo.

If you're going to live here, at least speak the language, James thought as he felt his blood start to rise. He raised his voice. "What? I didn't get that."

Joe suddenly jumped back as if startled—as if the English somehow assaulted him. He crept back from James, more than an arm's length distance, and shoved his hands into his pockets.

Despite himself, James looked down at the pot. Ugly in its simplicity, he decided to purchase it, or in other words, the words of four generations of traders before him, *trade*.

"I'll cut you a break." His voice melted into the sugary kindness of a salesman. "I'll give you, uh, four dollars for this. Take it or leave it."

Joe's eyes, a dark, muddy brown, stared at the floor as if the answer resided in the worn foot patterns in the carpet.

Again James took in a hasty shot of air and let it out

slowly. He didn't have all damn day. Freakin' people always late and slow...slow as molasses.

"Listen, you want the money or what?"

Joe nodded, again not speaking, and not for the first time, James wondered if the Navajo was too drunk or too simple to be doing business with. But the pot, although not his usual standard of workmanship, would fetch a retail price of at least a hundred dollars. He could sell it to tourists as authentic Navajo pottery—maybe even tell possible buyers the imperfections added charm to the piece and proved it wasn't mass produced. *Yeah, that will work out nicely.*

James went to the register and removed four, oily one-dollar bills. He reluctantly slapped them down on the table, greedily picked up the pot and hurriedly headed back to the stock room. He didn't hear Joe Yazzie leave, and he didn't care. His mind had already moved on to more important things like getting the new batch of kachinas to his retail stores in the Four Corners Area, Wild Sage, and Las Vegas.

It was well after six o'clock when James Tanner finally closed up shop for the night. The traffic on Route 66 had trickled down into a few mud splattered cars and trucks here and there. The train barreled through downtown as usual and it was the humming of the Santa Fe train that greeted him as he reached his own truck-a black F150.

Most of the other traders who had neighboring stores, had also closed up shop and the few that stayed open past six did so only on the hopes of snagging some tourists that were late getting into town.

He reached into his jeans pocket and took out his keys. To his surprise, he found the Navajo pot sitting upon the hood of his truck. He frowned. He knew he'd put that pot, that homely thing, on the stockroom shelf, while he pondered how best to sell it to the public.

But yet there it was—sitting on the hood of the truck as if demanding to be taken with him. James shook his head to clear the cobwebs and decided that he must've taken it out of the store with him without remembering.

He opened the doors, removed the pot from the hood and placed it in the passenger seat.

As he drove down Route 66, past the historic El Rancho Hotel and numerous other dives, the pot kept catching his eye, making him look at it for a few seconds before putting his gaze back on the road. He nearly wrecked twice and almost ran the curb when he finally turned off of Highway 66 and onto Aztec Avenue.

He made it home safely, but the pot kept drawing his attention. Amongst the multicolored turquoise, pink and orange patches there seemed to be a certain strangeness to it. It was almost as if expressions on the crudely carved lumps changed with each glance. They shifted, rearranging and then doing it all over again.

James decided it was the setting sun that tricked his eyes...nothing more.

He reached his house and pulled into the driveway. Shoving the truck into park, he twisted in the driver's seat toward the pot. It was a hideous thing, now that he got to thinkin' about it. How did he ever allow that Navajo to talk him into giving him four dollars for it?

But then another voice spoke up. He could hear it whispering in his ear and felt the words reverberate inside his skull. *You can sell it for more, like always.*

He laughed. Sure. Like all good traders, he never paid the natives anything near the actual retail price of their work.

James knew he could get at least a hundred dollars for it. Yeah, that's the thought he had early and had somehow forgotten. What was getting into him?

He climbed out of the truck, leaving the pot inside, and happily went into his well-furnished, ranch-style home. The profit margins were excellent so he could afford certain luxury. Most of the pottery he did buy or trade for, he bought terribly low and sold incredibly high. Such was the nature of capitalism and if the Navajo and the Zuni hadn't caught up with the times, then, well, too bad for them.

It was this motto that had fueled traders for decades, hell, even centuries. Of course, there were some honest ones, but James knew that they too bought as low as possible and sold the product very, very high. Tourists, especially those from Europe, ate it up with a thirst that didn't show any signs of being quenched. The higher the cost, the more turquoise, the more people thought the item was of value. Never mind that James had only paid fewer than twenty dollars for what he had sold for over a hundred.

———

J ames ate dinner (cheese enchiladas), watched the local basketball game and crawled into bed to sleep. He had plans for the pot tomorrow. The sooner he got rid of it the better. It gave him the creeps, but he wasn't willing to admit that to himself, or anyone else. The pot scared him on some deeper level, that crawled across his heart, and up into his mind.

After a few twists and turns, James finally slept.

Around midnight, a little bit after, James awoke. He sat upright in bed and with his eyes closed—listened.

He could've sworn he heard something.

James climbed out of bed, shoving his feet into well-worn slippers. He could've sworn he heard something that sounded an awfully like chanting—Indian chanting. *Damn drunk Indians stumbling down Aztec singing that unintelligible shit they call a language again...*James thought angrily.

Shuffling into the kitchen, he took two fingers, slipped them between the blinds and carefully peeked through. He secretly cursed. He looked out the windows and saw no one. No one passed out—no one wandering around the grounds, in fact, nothing moved at all. He let out a slow breath of relief. The police didn't need to be called. It was nothing.

Puzzled, but growing sleepy again, James started to turn back to his bedroom, but thought he'd better check the front of the house as well. He parted the blinds in the living room, noted how dusty they were, and peered across the front yard.

A shiny sliver of light caught his eye. He opened the blinds more and saw that the light came from his truck that was parked outside the garage.

He must've left the side door ajar or the interior light on.

"Damn it!" he hissed as he went to the kitchen, claimed his keys from the key holder and headed out into the cool night air.

As he reached the passenger side door, he heard chanting —a loud, hypnotic noise that drew him closer—not repelled him. Inside his inner voice screamed warnings, but James proceeded to unlock the door.

The pot's beaming glow only intensified the chanting. It grew louder and louder until James was sure the neighbors heard it. Still, he could not cover it up or smash it to the ground. He leaned in close to the item, the light forcing him to squint against its power.

"What in the hell?" he asked, to no one in particular.

The chanting of a thousand voices burrowed into his ears,

into his heart and into his head. The dashboard, the glove box and lastly the pot itself began to swirl around and James gripped the passenger door, his fingers turning white.

The light dragged his upper torso further into the car like he was a puppet. The words, the chanting became clear as he stared at the now clearly contorted faces on the pot.

Thief, thief, thief…

James frowned. Minutes before the language hadn't been anything close to English, more like—like Navajo, but now it had become painfully clear the word the faces spoke over and over again. Angry and unanimous the faces' chant continued to accuse him… *thief… thief… thief…*

Pulling back, James took in huge gulps of air as terror circled around his heart.

What was this thing? Whatever it was, it had to be destroyed. Freakin' Navajo witchcraft! Damn medicine men!

Carefully, his hands trembling, he picked up the hideous pot. As soon as his hands touched the bottom's clay base, burning pain shot through them. James screamed. The searing pain rushed into his psyche, blinding any logical thoughts and shooting the agony out into his entire body. He couldn't free his hands from the pottery— they were seared to the piece!

James screamed so loud and for so long he could no longer hear his own voice as the blackness swept onto him and pounced…like a thief.

———

At the corner of Aztec and Ford Canyon, Joe Yazzie stood with his head bent to the windy gusts that hurled from the New Mexican skyline—tossing even more dirt onto his already dusty clothes. Beneath the layers of dirt and grim, a smile shone from his dark, tanned face. The brim of his hat covered his midnight hair and his cowboy boots tapped on the sidewalk. The night's air was filled with petrified screams of terror that curled the toes and froze the heart.

Slowly, Joe walked over to the spot on the ground where the pot rested. He picked it up in his calloused hands and admired it under the moonlight. James Tanner's twisted expression of horror and angst stared blankly back at him.

Joe removed the four wrinkled dollars from his pocket and tossed them into the wind before removing an old, canvas sack from his jacket and placing the pot inside.

He laughed as the screams increased. He peered at James's terror-filled face. "Nice trade."

With the cackle of pure enjoyment, Joe vanished into the breeze.

The End

ONI SOARS

Worry surged in Oni's belly as she exited Chief Nnamdi's home. Tears threatened to blind her. She stumbled along the worn path, away from her home, away from her father, and the shocking news. The emotion evolved into fear, and it gnawed on her usual calm. As she hastened across the mesa, she could think of only one place to go, one place for answers, for solace—Kibwe's. As her priest and uncle, he would be able to soothe frustration her mother's news had caused.

Without waiting or announcing herself, as was customary, Oni barged into the main room of Kibwe's thatched roof home.

He got to his feet, concern staining his dark, wrinkled face. His hair, streaked with gray like the storm-coming sky, snaked outward in a halo of curls. The priest's aging shoulders sagged lower as he studied his niece's tear-stained cheeks.

"Oni? What's wrong?" He put down his pipe and crossed to her.

She shivered and tried to spit out the disgust. She failed.

"Come. Your spirit is unsettled." He took her hand and led her to the seat on the rug, close to the fire.

She didn't sit but struggled to breathe beneath the emotional boulder on her chest. Oni took another deep breath. "Moa is to have a child—a *male.*"

Moa, her mother, had been so happy when she told Oni. The emotional injury she inflicted had gone unnoticed.

Oni blew out her breath to ease the tightness in her chest at the memory. The child meant more than simply another life in their tribe. It meant the complete erasure of Oni as a person, as a living entity. So far, as the only child, she'd enjoyed her parents' affection and status within the village. No longer.

"I see." Kibwe fingered his prayer bag, containing mystic herbs and magic that hung around his neck.

How could he be so calm? Oni felt her heart was going to beat out of her chest, it thudded so.

He gazed into the fire. Along his left ear, smooth turquoise decorated his lobe. All priests wore these. Oni admired the jewelry, the magic, and the quiet power priests held. Her eyes moved down to the sacred bundle. It came from Tirawa, the Goddess, and was split into four sections. Each of the three priests held a bag containing a small piece of her body, with the largest fourth piece residing with the chief. When Kibwe died, his spirit would be reborn into a male child. Once grown, that man would take the bundle and become a priest. The cycle would continue as it had done since Tirawa formed from the mesa's orange clay.

"Come. Sit. We must think." Kibwe peered into the flames, reclaiming his pipe as he did so.

Following his example, Oni sat down, and retreated into meditation, emptying her mind of all her rambling, angry thoughts. She needed to collect her spirit. Rashness chased away peace and brought about chaos. And it was chaos that swirled around her mind now, stirring up turmoil and fear.

They often sat together for long stretches of time in muted silence. Ever since she could remember, Kibwe had been by her side. He didn't speak to her so much as listen to her body, her breathing.

After some time, Kibwe spoke.

"The child *will* be male. Ready yourself." His grave voice held the tone of one pronouncing the coming of a kin's death.

Oni nodded as a lump edged up her throat.

"The village needs a son—the *chief* needs a son—to carry his sacred bundle," Kibwe's face sagged as he spoke those words.

"You are certain it will be a male," Oni asked, her voice just above the fire's crackle.

Kibwe nodded.

"Who will carry your bundle?" Oni placed her hands in her lap. She'd asked him often, but he chose to not answer. It had become a sort of game between them.

Kibwe turned his head to the side and looked at her.

"I will carry yours," Oni said, smiling. She started to feel better, but only just. Kibwe's news didn't alleviate the situation, at all.

"The gods will decide." He turned back to the fire.

———

Time moved too quickly for Oni. Warm and lazy days of summer blended into the cool indifference of fall and into the cold, bitter arrival of winter. With the changes came celebrations. Soon, the chief would have a proper heir. Oni marked the growing, round bulge of her mother's belly with mounting dismay. Her father had all but stopped speaking to her. She'd become like the wind—invisible.

So, she spent much of her free time as she always had—with Kibwe.

One bleak afternoon, with the desert sky clouded over and blotting out the sun's rays, they walked amongst the homes and farms sprinkled across the valley floor. A thin layer of snow covered the ground. High above them, Onawa Mesa overlooked the farmers. Only the chief and his family, priests, and servants could live on the mesa, so close to their ancestors, the stars.

"The weather is cold, but hardly wet. There will be a great famine." Kibwe pointed up to the pregnant sky and clutched his blanket tight around his aging body. "Look! The Great Sky, Tirawa, does not release her water to us. Little water means little food."

Oni followed the direction of Kibwe's finger. The sacred mountains off in the distance didn't have their usual snow caps.

"We can do the water dance."

"Perhaps." Kibwe's voice betrayed his disbelief.

As was their ritual, he didn't say more, but found a large rock, jutting up from the ground. He sat, his breathing labored from their descent down the mesa and subsequent walk through the valley.

Oni climbed up beside him.

As moments ticked by, she pondered the politics of the gods. She rested her head on her knees.

After a while, Kibwe broke the silence. "When the time comes, the water dance will not be enough. I fear the gods are angry."

Kibwe's words contradicted the other two priests' opinion. The gods would soon bless the village with a male child.

In the spring, the Koma River flooded and the canals brimmed with water.

Much time had passed since those warm, wet days.

Was this the reason Kibwe wanted to take a walk in this frigid weather?

Oni didn't say this to Kibwe. Instead, she asked, "What have we done to anger them?"

"Your father's ungratefulness has upset the great Sky, Tirawa. She has blessed our village for many years. Chief Nnamdi doesn't see how much he's been given. Only when he learned your mother was with child did he begin to celebrate and make sacrifices to Tirawa."

"Does he know?"

Kibwe nodded. "Imamu and Akakios disagreed. Your father's priests only care to please him, but they lack true sight. I told Chief Nnamdi of this as well, and he laughed."

Oni shook her head in disbelief. As the eldest priest, Kibwe held more knowledge than the others, but in recent years, the chief had taken to heeding Imamu's and Akakios' advice.

"A famine?" Oni shuddered. The wind blew icy cold across her blanket-clad shoulders.

"Yesterday, I sought answers in the smoke. This is what it told me. Imamu and Akakio plot not only his death, but—"

"We must share this with the great warriors! To warn my parents..."

Kibwe stared at her with watery eyes. "Oni, my time grows short on the mesa and my final journey into the great Sky approaches. You must tell no one of our words this day. For the moment, all is well, but be mindful, Oni."

"But, Kibwe!"

"Silence!" His frail body shook from his effort. "No questions. Only listen. You must walk between fields to soothe Tirawa."

"Only males walk between fields."

Kibwe gave her a sobering look. "Women have always saved this village, from the wounds they mend, to the food they cook, to sound counsel wives give husbands. Bravery knows no gender."

A Walker must possess both the nature and strength to carry the sacred bundle across the sky, between the fields of the mesa and the fields of the heavens. Securing the Great Hawk's feather demonstrated skills in climbing, negotiating, and cunning. A Walker would also be charged with grabbing the hide of a mythical snake. This demonstrated bravery and integrity, for he would have to avoid being poisoned by the snake's fangs and words. At last, he must convince the Sun God to anoint his skin—a feat that often proved the resiliency of the Walker and his kinship with the stars.

By doing so, he demonstrated to his kin and the elders that he came from the stars. Every member of their village knew this lore. It had been the Sky God's words to Star Man and Star Woman. Oni tucked her chin to her knees and rocked forward.

Kibwe spoke until the velvety night covered the horizon. Under the still twinkling eyes of their forefathers who had taken up residence with the Sky God, Kibwe told Oni of future things and past things. Most importantly he told her of present things—and that frightened her the most.

———

Months later, as the first sprigs of spring burst through the desert ground, Oni's mother gave birth to Baako. The village and Chief Nnamdi celebrated the glorious blessing with feasts, dances, and gifts to the Sky God.

Oni didn't participate—neither did Kibwe. They remained in his home. He lay on a flat woven mat, his face covered in sweat. Blankets covered him, but Kibwe still complained of being cold.

"The room roasts!" Oni wiped his face with a cloth. She passed him a cup of water. "Drink."

He took a few brief sips before descending into a coughing fit that rocked his narrow frame with such violence that Oni had to hold him down or else he'd roll into the fire.

While the rest of the village danced, drank, and dedicated food to the gods, Oni tried to heal Kibwe. He'd lost so much moisture that he resembled a dried out stick with skin stretched over his bones.

She clutched Kibwe's skinny hand in hers and she squeezed. "Let me go for the priests. Please. Imamu and Akakios can—"

"They can do nothing!" Kibwe coughed.

"But..."

"Do not be afraid. Be strong. You know the path the gods have cleared for you. Take it."

With trembling hands, he untied the sacred bundle from his neck, and pushed it into Oni's hand. He slumped back onto the mat and closed his eyes. Behind his shut lids, Kibwe's eyes fluttered, and then fell still.

"Kibwe?" Oni shook him, gently at first, and then harder, as panic clutched her heart. "Kibwe!"

He did not stir.

She pushed the sacred bundle into her dress's pocket. He

had left her and fled to the Sky to be with their ancestors. Her sorrow seeped out of her eyes, but the loss took up residence in her heart.

———

The Sunning time returned. In the midst of the endless string of hot days, Oni took up her water baskets and climbed down to the Koma River. Others made the trek—all women, for males did not draw their own water.

During her tenure with Kibwe in the winter, Oni had woven herself many water baskets. Kibwe's directions had been clear.

You must be sure to prepare, even if at first there appears to be no sign of a famine. You will need to be strong to walk between the fields, Oni...

Once Oni reached the edge of the Koma, she noticed she could see the brownish orange edge of the dirt-like clay. It had never been this low.

"The Sun God has stretched out his hand to the mountains to provide water to feed the Koma. So why does the river not swell to its fullest?" A young woman balanced one of her water baskets on her head.

"The winter was brief, the Koma has not been properly fed, and the gods are angry" answered another, an elderly woman with wild gray hair and bright eyes.

"Then we will not be properly fed. Take as much as you need for your family and sheep," Oni added.

"Who are you to tell us what to do? You are no priest. You lack power to see the future." The young woman scowled at Oni, but Oni only smiled thinking of the bundle hidden in the folds of her dress.

The other women added their noise to her comments.

"I am the daughter of Chief Nnamdi and a daughter of Tirawa!"

The elderly woman adjusted her basket and pursed her lips.

Oni searched the women's faces. They melded from young to old, but all carried the same conditioning of their tribe, demanding women silence their tongues and still their anger in the presence of men.

Baako's birth had brought renowned celebration, but it had also conjured sorrow. Moa had died two days after his arrival. Every woman knew the cost that came with giving birth and the sacrifices it entailed. Mothers had given all for men, sometimes even their lives.

Ignoring the hot, angry buzzing of the women around her, Oni got to her knees, removed the baskets from her back, and gathered water. Once done, and with two of the heavy water baskets on her back, and another slung over her shoulder, she climbed back up the mesa. She thought of her mother. Most women fetched the water, but not Moa. Servants performed that duty for her. Now, she slept with her ancestors in the sky. Oni's heart ached in grief. Moa had never been warm toward her. Oni wondered if her presence reminded Moa of her shame in not bearing a male first. Moa encouraged Oni spend time with Kibwe and away from her. Despite this, Moa taught Oni how to make a braid, how to sew, and how to start a fire.

As she rounded the corner to her home, which had once been Kibwe's, Imamu stepped in her path.

"Stop!" His two thick braids gleamed under the sun's rays, making his hair look like poisoned water.

"Speak quickly, for the Sun God's power does not relent." Oni put down one of her water baskets.

Imamu stiffened at her words. He gazed down at her, drawing himself up to his full height. "Do you command the priests now, young Oni? I am not Kibwe, nor am I easily bent to your whims."

"It doesn't take the light of the Sun God to show everyone that you are no *Kibwe*," Oni retorted.

"As I have mentioned before, it doesn't do for a chief's daughter to reside outside his home or for woman to live in the priest's house. For a woman to live alone without a male companion is also taboo…as you well know."

"Kibwe had no heirs, save me. His home is within my family's right to claim. So I do."

"I will speak with your father about this continued disrespect."

"As you see fit," Oni replied.

Imamu touched the bundled sack hanging from his neck. "You continue to defy your father's orders to return Kibwe's bundle. Give it to me."

If she gave it to Imamu, the equality of power would tip to favor him.

"No."

"You wish another beating?" Imamu couldn't hide his surprise.

"No. Kibwe trained me. I'm a priest and I won't be beaten." Oni opened her door and went inside to escape the heat. She placed her water baskets down before turning to Imamu, who had followed her inside.

"For a priest, you seem not to be aware of the common values of respect. You enter my home without asking." Oni met his eyes.

Imamu waved off her comments. "The gods demand the return of the bundle."

"Then you are a god? Are you so proud as to sit *beside* Tirawa and not at her feet?" Oni shook her head. "You come here seeking nothing but *power*. Had Kibwe meant for you to have the bundle, he would have given it to you."

"You dare defy a priest's home with your stink? You're a *woman*." Imamu sneered. "You're nothing but a piece for bartering. Cleverness is not for *womenfolk*. Kibwe contaminated your thoughts and misled you. You may find yourself dead, rather than rewarded."

"You cannot stop the Sky."

"We'll see." Imamu clucked his tongue for emphasis.

"Won't we?" Oni said.

He searched her face, and then with one last scowl, left.

———

As Kibwe had predicted, a famine hit the village— gradually, but by the beginning of the Falling season, some had grown weak and died. The priests performed their ceremonies to make the rain come, but their sacrifices and prayers went unheeded.

Baako grew, but was no older than a few months when the full force of the famine descended. On the mesa, the royal family and priest continued to eat and drink well. But on the valley floor, people and herds starved.

After the first snow, more than half of the people in the valley had died. The farmers came to her father's home and told him of death and desperation that ran rampant among them.

Chief Nnamdi stated, "There's no danger. Save the water you use and split it between yourself and your herd."

Oni stood at the rear of the farmers' group.

"When you feel the stabbing pangs of hunger, then you'll see!" one farmer shouted.

"Speak of this no more. Go to your homes, your families,

and use the water wisely." Chief Nnamdi turned to go.

One farmer folded his hands into tight fists. "When will you notice us and not your *son*!"

The other farmers exited their session with the chief, dragging their dead comrade with them—her father's blade buried to the hilt in his chest. The chief's swift temper knew no limit.

The farmers spoke of caring for their families and animals. They would give him no more words. They would also no longer provide food to the mesa, only for their people below, they vowed. Oni couldn't believe her father's blind indifference. He *had* to do something before the famine became worse.

No. *She* had to do something.

Moving with the mass of farmers, she headed for her own residence. Kibwe's predictions had come true, but how could she help save the people her father ignored? Already so many had died.

"Oni," Chief Nnamdi called.

She froze. He hadn't spoken to her in nearly a year. According to the servants, he'd become so enthralled with his son, he rarely spoke to anyone.

She turned to face him, kneeling in respect. "Chief Nnamdi."

They were alone. Father and daughter. Two strangers.

"You seem different." He gestured for her to stand.

"I have grown." Oni stood but didn't close the distance between them.

"Yes. Kibwe's death hurt you. Maybe that is what's changed you. Imamu says you are defiant and disrespectful. You continue to refuse my orders to return the bundle and to move out of his home. I'm sure Kibwe did not teach you these things."

"Kibwe taught me other things. The first was not to believe Imamu."

"Speak no more ill of him, child."

"I am no child." Oni's anger uncoiled like a snake within her.

Her father flinched before catching himself.

"You dare speak to me—your chief, as well as your father —in this manner? Imamu is correct. Your insolence knows no bounds."

"As does yours! People are *dying*. What will you do to appease the gods?"

"The people are spoiled from years of plenty. There is still enough."

"Walk around the village! Visit the people in the valley! They're starving."

"You speak untruths! Did Kibwe teach you nothing?" Chief Nnamdi barked.

"He taught me everything! You are not worthy to speak his name!"

The chief backhanded Oni to the ground. "I am still your chief and your father!"

Oni rose to her feet, pain throbbing in her face.

"I am no daughter of yours."

Before he could strike her again, she stalked out. Her father's outraged shouts chased after her.

Once home, she started the fire and emptied her mind of all thoughts. In the flames, all would be revealed if one was willing to hear.

Oni sat, breathed slowly, and listened.

———

A nother month passed, and the people of the mesa began to grumble like those of the valley. The wailing grief of a people dying grew louder still. Oni, who had devoted one of the three rooms in Kibwe's home to stock-piling food, shared it with others. The people saw her as healthy and, when she walked among them, found her a welcome resource. She knew how to nurture plants and how to encourage them to grow.

One bitterly cold night, Oni sat alone at her fire eating a roast rabbit.

"Oni, it is Imamu. I am coming in. Call out if you object."

"Come."

Once inside, he inhaled the air. "It smells good in here."

Oni didn't speak.

"Several of the elders are meeting. Your presence is requested."

"By whom?"

"Your father." With nothing further, Imamu left.

Oni collected the sacred bundle from its hiding place. She tied it around her neck. Instantly, she felt Kibwe with her. *It is time. Time for all to know her true calling.* Instead of feeling nervous, as she had thought she might, the bundle steadied her spirit.

Oni reached her father's home to find a crowd—it appeared to be everyone in the village—circling around it. The bundle around her neck began to glow and pulsate as she walked. Oni parted the sea of people as a fire does darkness.

She stopped short outside the entrance to her father's home.

"Chief Nnamdi, I'm here." The bundle grew brighter.

Whispers sprung up at her words.

"She is not a priest! Who is she to wear the sacred

bundle?"

Yet another shouted, "She's a woman!"

The three most powerful men in the village came out. One by one their eyes fell on the bundle around Oni's neck. They shielded their eyes, squinting against her power.

Akakios spoke first, for he was a good speaker of words. "The gods have ignored our prayers and our sacrifices! They're angered and punish us! The sacred bundle must be returned to a true priest for our suffering to end!"

The people cheered and thrust Oni forward.

Akakios lay out his palm. "Give it to me."

"You speak only lies." Oni stepped back, but the crowd pushed her forward again.

"It glows in fury." Akakios gestured to her neck.

"It glows in outrage at your actions!" Oni shouted back.

The crowd rose up in. Loud jeering and screaming filled the night air.

"Liar!"

"Heretic!"

"Silence her!"

She turned to her father. "The gods need to be appeased. Let me go to them."

The bundle's pulsation increased as if agreeing.

Oni turned to face the people. "Your priests have turned the gods away from our village."

Again the group of villagers roared their denials.

At last Chief Nnamdi spoke. "Silence! We need a Walker."

"We need a Walker!" someone shouted, and others around him agreed.

Imamu came forward, dark eyes narrowed. "Your son is too young to walk the fields."

Chief Nnamdi nodded, but he kept his eyes on Oni. "She is not."

It took a few moments for Oni to heed his words. He *believed* her. Maybe it was because the situation involved the death of so many people. Maybe because his son was also endangered. Maybe he believed in Kibwe's words.

It didn't matter—he *believed*.

"What we need is to raid the villages to the east!" roared a huge man with a thick neck and muscular chest. He raised his spear into the air and a small group of men around him shouted agreement.

Chief Nnamdi shook his head. "We will not risk further anger from the gods by taking from others."

A louder group rallied behind *his* words.

Oni seized the moment. "I am first born and the Walker Between Fields. As the Walker I can collect the three sacred items to give to the great creator, Tirawa."

A groan and furious shouts rose high into the night air, beating against Oni's back.

Chief Nnamdi addressed the mass of people. "The sacred bundle should have killed her. Kibwe trusted her and selected her instead of a male to learn the ways of a priest."

"And now we die for it!"

Murmurs whipped across the people like a wild fire across the desert valley below, starting slow, and then rushing into a raging crescendo of sound.

"We will consult the gods. Elders, meet with me inside," Chief Nnamdi declared.

Four men came forward and followed the chief into his home.

Oni waited with bated breath, but kept her back to the door, facing the people. Tension crawled across her skin. Her father's warrior guard remained alert.

That didn't ease her fear. Oni tried to calm the raging

storm of emotions that whipped and roared about inside her. The glowing of the sacred bundle lessened, as if it too was unsure. Her heart seemed to stutter and halt, and she had to keep reminding herself to breathe. Murmurs, scorching and fearful, swirled around her.

The moments stretched on, twisting and tangling into a mangled web of doubt.

Oni suddenly heard Kibwe's gentle, careful voice in her ear—as if the breeze carried it down from the heavens.

You are a Walker Between Fields.

As if hearing Kibwe's words, Chief Nnamdi emerged, the trail of elderly men behind him. Oni let out a slow, unsteady breath. The group of villagers became silent.

Chief Nnamdi's solemn face seemed to have aged a thousand years in the time he'd held counsel. He glanced across the masses, pausing briefly, before allowing his eyes to finally rest on Oni.

"Walker Between Fields, the elders have decided. You must retrieve the three sacred items to save our village from the gods' rage."

Oni's ears rang as the words vibrated deep inside. "Yes... yes, Chief Nnamdi. Yes, Father!"

"The gods will kill us all! She is a *woman!*" An elderly man raised his fist and shook it.

Several others joined in, and soon shouts, cries, and all-out wails saturated the air.

"Enough!" Chief Nnamdi roared. "Our people are *dying*! This is our chance to make peace with the gods! You, who are so certain of our demise, go! Jump to your deaths! The mesa's edge is there!" He pointed to the cliff. "But don't whine and wail like sheep before a slaughter!"

He turned to Oni. With a smile he said, "Save our people, my daughter."

Tears burned in her eyes.

"I will."

The elders remained silent, their lips pursed together as if they disagreed with the chief's decision but had been unable to say so. Her father's words burned true—the village had no choice.

"Then go," her father said, his eyes wet with unshed tears. He coughed to clear his throat. "Return to us with victory on your breath."

———

A s the new day broke—innocent and unknowing— Walker Between Fields stepped over the edge of the mesa where many thought she'd drop to her death. Yet the gods were with her, and she bounced up from the valley floor, toward the sky, reaching for Tirawa to catch her. She released the sacred wind from the bundle. Flying high on its power, she disappeared into the horizon.

Many believed she died. No one survived a fall over the edge. After all, she was *female.* Search parties went out to return Oni's body, but when they returned empty handed, the villagers said that she had probably survived her fall, but had run off rather than admit her defeat.

As for Chief Nnamdi, he retreated into his home. Two warrior guards stood outside the entrance. No one entered and no one left.

The people of Onawa worried.

They had good reason.

Much had been placed in Oni's hands. Some wept and counted themselves dead.

Others held out hope that the Sky God knew exactly what she was doing.

D ays blurred into each other like a well-woven blanket with no sight of the Walker Between Fields. People continued to perish. Panic and fear covered the village. Chief Nnamdi hadn't been seen. Some said he had fallen on his spear in shame. Others said he sat behind his walls, eating and drinking while others starved.

Suffering raged on.

One day, after a long morning of burying their dead, a group of villagers met outside Kibwe's old home. Today, they would demolish the hut, ridding the village of the memories.

Overhead and without warning, the clouds thickened. So sudden the change, people stopped.

A silhouette soared above them, breaking the monotony of clouds. Thunderous shouts of joy coaxed Chief Nnamdi from his home. He shielded his eyes against the brightness.

Above, the Walker Between Fields descended—she who had been Oni.

"She comes! She comes!" the people exclaimed.

Walker Between Fields's feet landed softly on the mesa. The wind folded from her with a *whoosh*. She had retrieved the hawk's feather. Her deep brown skin glowed despite the absence of the sun. An aura gleamed around her, as if the Sun God had stained her skin during her journey between the beyond. Legends spoke of that place where the world and time joined.

Amazed, the crowd parted as she gracefully walked forward. As she did so, people dropped to their knees—heads bowed, either from her power or from the immense brightness of her aura.

As Walker Between Fields strolled among them, her gaze

—stony in her unsmiling face—did not waver from Chief Nnamdi's.

When she reached him, at the rear of the masses, she passed the items she carried to him. She smelled of flowers, dirt, and trees. With trembling hands, he took them, holding them close to his chest. He opened his lips to speak, but faltered.

Walker Between Fields said, "I have returned with the great hawk's feather, the snake's hide, and my skin that shines from the Sun god's blessing. I have walked between fields and earned the gods' favor. Your people, *our* people, will suffer no more."

"Liar!" someone shouted and the murmurs grew.

"Still your tongues!" Walker Between Fields ordered.

As she did so, the first splats of rain fell onto the thirsty earth. Faster they fell quieting the naysayers and astounding the believers. Soon, people erupted in praise to the great Sky God and to the Walker Between Fields.

Like the heavens, Oni's father's tears spilled over. "Come, stand with me, for you have rescued us all."

Walker Between Fields took her place beside her father until the end of his days.

The End

THE WICKED WILD

"A wind can move the branches of trees, but it will never move the head of a man."

--African Proverb

1901
New Mexico Territory

"Who there?" Zara Gibson whirled toward the sound. "Come on out here now!"

The gods grew up in the foothills of this place. In the gods' shadows, hills, mesas, and arroyos remained, or so the Navajo believed. The gusts of wind swept through the valley between the natural monuments.

The wind didn't silence the crunch of footsteps.

She waited.

One breath.

Two breaths.

Three breaths.

The wind died as if listening too. Nothing. She resumed

her walk along the untamed path toward home. A body couldn't be too careful.

Out here, the West wasn't just wild.

It was wicked.

Zara suspected the wickedness had found Chad Wilkins. A prick of anger fed by the heavy loss of the Civil War. She'd spied him fooling around in some arroyo consumed by thick billowing smoke, but no fire. She'd smelled the odor of spoiled eggs, thick like the smoke, and took off. With her heart pounding, she prayed he hadn't caught her spying.

Not that she meant to be spying. She had been out walking to get some fresh air—until it turned foul.

"How come you ain't got your black ass to town to do the laundry?" Chad asked as he emerged from the brush. She spied his horse appearing behind him as if a dark apparition.

He spat around the wad of tobacco from his mouth. The cowboy hat, dirt brown from years of wear and weather, cast his eyes in shadow. His horse looked away, embarrassed by his owner's lack of tact.

Zara picked up the scattering of dried tumbleweed around her appropriated hogan, giving her hands something to keep busy. Idle hands became the Devil's workshop, and Zara had one devil too many standing in front of her.

"Ya hear me?" Chad shouted. Soon the deep rattling of his cough shook his body and choked off whatever other vile he intended to spew.

Zara stopped and turned to face him. "I hear ya talkin'."

"You ain't been in a week."

Zara took in a breath and released it. "Been down in my spirit."

Chad scowled. "I ain't brought you all the way out here for you to get lazy."

"I brought myself. Earned my own way. Walked on my own two feet. An' I ain't felt too good."

The whole point of coming out to this land and settling was to be free of folks like Chad, men who thought they still owned her and her people.

Chad peered across to her the way folks looked at scorpions scurrying across the road. His dark green eyes narrowed. "I protected ya."

Zara adjusted her headscarf. "Say you."

"So, getcha black ass back to town before I drag you back," Chad said.

Zara put her chapped hands on her hips. She didn't miss the washing and scrubbing. The harsh lye soap ate into her skin and even now, days later, her hands still bore welts and angry flesh. She looked him up and down before shaking her head. *Some people just don't know how they sound.*

"I go to town when I'm good an' ready. I ain't yo slave no more."

Chad spat out another wad of tobacco. It sounded like coughing out a hairball—wet and dark. It landed near her skirt. He wiped his mouth with the back of his hand and shrugged like her words didn't matter.

They did.

And she knew it.

"You see, *girl*, just 'cause we living in the new frontier don't mean we like being dirty. We're civilized, not savages."

Zara peered harder against the glint of the sinking New Mexico sun. The wide-brimmed cowboy hat cast his face all in shadow, except the slash of anger on his lips. This close to dusk, the leaving light revealed the slivers of smoke escaping from Chad's back, smoke that the ordinary folk wouldn't see. Could be trick of the light. Could be trick of the devil.

"No point in being clean when your soul's stained black," Zara said.

"You know all about being black, don't you? How many good people died 'cause of your kind? And for what?" Chad scratched at the beard crawling along his jawline. "Lazy good-for-nothin'."

Zara didn't give a direct answer. She'd traveled far, across hard, unyielding earth to get to what some called the Promised Land. She wouldn't waste time on the likes of him. With a sigh, she turned to go inside her home.

The cocking of a gun caught her attention, and she turned back to him.

"You don't turn your back to me." Chad pointed his pistol in anger. "That's enough damn disrespect, you filthy n…"

On instinct, Zara lifted her hands and with palms out, swept them upward, toward the heavens. A huge gust of wind rushed over Chad. The language of her forefathers and foremommas rushed in a stream of verbal magic. She commanded the winds, and they readily obeyed.

The blood in her connected to all that came before. They took their payment from her, payment for her calling them out and waking them. They always left her tired. So tired.

Sometimes, it was worth it.

Like now.

"Come, great winds!" She commanded the wind to whirl around him. The roaring of the blood in her body spoke to her fury, and it called to theirs. Pent up anger from years of enslavement, cruelty, and torment had unfurled.

Chad's lips puckered. Eyes bulging, he clawed at his neck trying to ease the pressure on his windpipe. The winds stole his breath. His face became a dark purple, and he'd drawn blood in thin rivulets along his neck before Zara lowered her fists.

"You a nasty person, Chad Wilkins." Zara coughed out blood, thick and wet like the tobacco wad now drying on the parched earth. Zara wiped her mouth. She didn't like using it, the magic. Not because of the damage to her own spiritual core, but because it frightened folks.

And frightened folks did foolish things.

She peered at him, the roar of power burning in her palms' centers. The skin along Chad's temple bulged outward and crawled down to his mouth. He opened it and spew of black smoke shot out. Zara raised her hand and wind rose up to whisk it away.

Chad cackled, but behind his eyes, Zara saw something *other*.

With her chest burning in agony, she waved her hand, and a whispered, "Thank you," to her ancestors. To Chad, she said, "Go on now, Chad. Y'all leave me be."

Chad gasped, his inhales rattling in a wet, sickening manner. He coughed out some words in her direction, before yanking on the reins and leaving, just as she had wanted. The red-purple hue had started to fade, but the damage to his windpipe would take days, maybe weeks, to heal.

As he left, he wheezed out three words. "You. Gonna. Pay."

Zara sighed. Now she'd done it. The wickedness would come for her. The movement behind Chad's eyes and rippling beneath his skin didn't belong there. The very thing she had hoped to avoid by relocating to this desolate place, she had angered.

The devil would have his due.

And clean laundry.

———

T rouble arrived first thing in the morning.

Throughout the previous evening, the wind's howling had warned of approaching evil. Despite the pain and soreness in her muscles, she'd risen early, heeding her ancestors' wisdom, and found Sheriff Hicks waiting outside her door, his fist raised to knock. He didn't have his usual smile.

Sheriff Hicks tipped his hat, but didn't enter. He hesitated, then said, "Understand me fully, Zara. Chad Wilkins come to see me last night. Now, I dunno what happened. You can't just go around attacking folks. This ain't some juju village in Africa. We might be living in a wilderness, but we observe the social graces of life. I won't stand for base savagery in Wild Sage..."

Zara listened, allowing Hicks to say his piece. He was the law, after all.

Men like Chad looked strong, but that strength didn't go all the way through. Just on the surface. She suspected Chad had taken it bad, but it went deeper than hurting his feelings. The *other* inside him, housed up in his body, recognized her power, and that of her ancestors. It wanted it, craved it.

But Sheriff Hicks didn't wanna hear 'bout all that.

So, she crossed her arms. "He drew on me."

Sheriff Hicks climbed back onto his horse and leaned over his saddle. "What did you do to make him do that, Zara?"

She sighed. "Sheriff, I done lived a bunch of places, and the land always changes. Sumthin' that don't always change —*hate*. Whether it be here or in the deepest hell of Mississippi, the wickedness don't care. It feeds on the hate."

Sheriff Hicks's breath shuddered. "Look here, Zara. I'm a Christian, so I don't believe in that mojo stuff. All I got was a battered cowpoke crying foul. Dunno how you did it, or even if you did it. Just stay away from him. Okay?"

"I'm a freed person. No more master. No more followin' orders."

"You still gotta follow the law."

"What about him? What about the pistol he drew on me? Threatened my life! He didn't even tell you that."

"You sayin' it's self-defense?"

"I'm sayin' he's the lowest value of a coward, drawin' on me when my back's turned. If he come out here again and tries to take my life, he won't be comin' to talk to you about it." Zara crossed her arms.

As she stood just outside threshold of her residence, she studied the broad-shouldered lawman. He rode a dark horse. The tan cowboy hat kept the sun from his face. His gun belt slung low over his hips contained his guns, and his badge shone from his chest. Wiry and red-haired with spectacles, he didn't look like danger. A mistake that many numbered dead had made.

"I see. You like getting your own way, don't you, Zara?" Hicks rubbed his chin. Then, his usual smile emerged on his lips.

She shrugged. "Don't ever'body?"

"Indeed." He laughed.

"Changes are shiftin' things, Sheriff. The wickedness ain't gonna lie still. It be comin'. Sum folks better be gettin' used to that."

He studied her for a moment, before shaking his head. "What you goin' on about? More of that juju?"

She fixed her gaze on him. "Sumthin's here and that little pistol ain't gonna help."

"Ain't no problem these guns can't solve, Zara." He patted the butt of a gun, but his smile sagged a little. "Now, will you just come into town and wash? The unmarried menfolk like going to church with clean clothes. Might find 'em a good God-fearin' woman."

———

The sound of wagons and galloping horses couldn't drown out the saloon's music next door from filtering into the laundry. She could smell the alcohol and unwashed bodies sweating off their drunk over the scent of the lye. Despite being early in the day, laughter and howls emitted in concert with the music of frontier life. Inside the store, she sat perched on the stool as the water-filled cauldrons warmed over the fire. Beyond the buildings, the blistering and scorched landscape stretched out across the New Mexico territory.

That morning Zara ate her breakfast and walked back into town with the morning sun accompanying her as it rose higher in the heavens. Some townspeople called the land enchanted. Spirits rose from the ground and inhabited the trees, the animals, and the stars. The sky birthed humans and all living things. Here, the line between reality and mystery blurred. How else did you describe the towering mesas, the deep canyons, and magical terrain? One thing was certain. Living in this wilderness wore down lives. She saw it in the eyes of customers who came to get their clothes washed. All men. Single. Widowers.

It'd been three days since Chad Wilkins's visit. Recovered, Zara stood on the storefront's porch, attempting to catch the breeze. Already, the New Mexico sun wrought high heat and little relief. The mile trek into town had been slow, but she got there.

"Ah, you finally drag your sorry ass into town!" Chad

leered as he stumbled out of the saloon. The inky smoke drifted from him and his shadow shimmered as if unable to hold the shape.

Zara tried to ignore him. *It.* She shifted her eyes instead to the beautiful mesa beyond him, but the smoke skewed her view. No one else on the street—those strolling past, those standing around talking—seemed to be able to see the wickedness that had claimed Chad Wilkins.

"You hear me?" Chad roared.

"Yeah. Ever'body can hear you." Zara turned to go back inside her shop. Maybe he'd knock off and return to the abandoned hogan, back to his demonic master, or he'd follow her in, which would at least take him away from those on the street.

His bellowing drew a crowd from the saloon. Several people paused as they strolled along to observe the antics of the town idiot.

Darn it! That's what she didn't want—a group of folks in danger of getting hurt if Chad's *other* decided to engage her.

"That's 'cause I got somethin' to say to you! Witch!"

Zara paused inside her store. The wind whistled as it slipped in. Yes, she heard the warning. Chad and the others moved down the short porch toward her.

"Sheriff Hicks let you off. You should be in a jail, woman." Chad spat out the word *woman* as if it had been a curse. "I betcha bewitched him too. I can see it in ya even if they don't." Tendrils of dark smoke spiraled from the corners of his mouth as he leered at her.

The crowd, now gathered at her door, shuddered in unison. Hot and fast whispers whipped about them, chasing after Chad's words. Zara put her hands on her hips, but held her peace.

"You deny you did this?" Chad pointed at his neck, the contusion still visible, but fading.

"Quit your bellyaching. You got your ass kicked by a woman." Bud chided from just behind Chad, before elbowing his way to the front. He tipped back his cowboy hat. "Belly back up to the bar and drink your sorrow like ever'body else."

"She's a filthy witch! I tell you." Chad repeated. His face flushed.

Zara watched as the flush deepened to black blotches blossoming along his cheeks, across his forehead, and down into his beard. The hard green of his eyes turned dark. His hands sported long, beastlike claws.

No one else noticed.

Right before her, the wickedness consumed the rest of Chad's humanity.

"Eh, yeah! She's made the dirt on my Sunday shirt disappear!" shouted Rancher John.

Laughter.

From the rear someone added, "Aye, ain't that magic!"

More laughter.

It ripped through the group, cresting in volume before tapering off as members tired of the fun and turned back toward the saloon. The noonday sun made one thirsty.

Zara suppressed her smile but glowed inside at their kind words about her washing skills. It failed to eclipse the mounting fear inside her. Already her hands tingled in anticipation. The being inside Chad may attack now, or wait. Most of the time, devils did things in the dark, under the cover of night, when man's defenses were low.

Chad shoved Bud away, still fixing Zara with a glare. There it was, the hot gaze of the other inside him, the wickedness that puppeted him. She'd seen that look on many a frustrated white man's face. He'd meant to cause her strife, but that had failed.

The man wanted to make her pay for that. The demon wanted to feast on what remained.

She shuddered at the truth in that thought.

With the words of her ancestors in her ear and her heart, the voices of her grandm0mma spoke of their strength. *Do not fear. We are one.*

"Leave. I have work to do." Zara nodded toward the saloon.

Chad grunted, made a rude gesture, and stormed off, the angry dark wickedness flowing behind him like a cape.

———

D usk. Few people remained on the road. Most had retired to their homes and families. Even the saloon next door had intermittent periods of silence. Shoulders singing in fatigue, hands raw from the lye, and back throbbing from lifting and bending, Zara longed for a hot cup of coffee and a comfortable bed.

She'd just closed the door when Chad Wilkins appeared in the road.

"You whore! Witch!" he yelled. He clutched two lanterns, one in each hand. The flames inside each held an eerie and otherworldly green flame.

"Go home, Chad. Just walk on back to where you came from," Zara warned. The hair on the back of her neck stood up.

"You know what they used to do with witches?" Chad bellowed, spittle flying.

He raised the lanterns high in the air.

Chad hurled the first one at her.

She fell backward against the door. With swift hands, she turned the knob and raced inside. The lantern missed her but slammed into the store's wall, bursting and sending the green fire and oil all over.

"You fool!" Zara screamed as the second one shot past.

Fire latched onto the wooden structure as fast as lightning. It chewed, not just her store, but soon the saloon next door, too. Dry air and even drier wood burned encouraging the flames. Growing every second, the flames spread—greedy and propelled by the desert's high winds. Billows of smoke wafted into the sky and back into Zara's store.

"Fire! Fire!" Screams rose into a chorus.

Blinded by smoke, Zara crouched down to get air. On her knees, she crawled out the door and off the porch. Fear spread as fast as the fire itself to the few who remained in town.

Chad disappeared into the smoke and falling light.

"What happened?" Sheriff Hicks met Zara in the center of the road.

"Chad," Zara coughed out.

"Water! Get water! Form a line from the arroyo!" Sheriff Hicks shouted at a group of men racing from the smoking saloon.

Horrible wickedness ravaged one building, skipping in delight from one wooden area to the other, greedily consuming all in its path.

That's what the Devil came to do. Kill. Steal. Destroy.

The harshness of ignorance and hate may have come to the West, but Zara and her ancestors wouldn't let this promised land be destroyed by it.

No.

What to do? She'd just recovered from her last attempt to

fight off Chad Wilkins. That had been in anger, and the fury rolled forward in her even now.

The Indians could call down the rain, but it was her African ancestors who controlled the wind. Even as she pulled from her inner strength, the fire began to fan back toward the already charred sections, lowering the heat. The magic pulled on her life force, and she coughed, bloody spittle dark and wet against the dirt road. She got to her feet, her lungs burning. Her ancestors had blessed her. The winds had calmed the flames. The townspeople raced to put out what remained of the blaze.

"Thank God the whole damn town didn't burn." Sheriff Hicks clapped a hand on her shoulder. "You all right?"

"That's twice Chad tried to kill me." The burning lessoned as the wind calmed around her.

"You sure it was him?"

"I got two eyes, Sheriff."

"All right. All right." He put his hands on his guns. "I'll bring him in."

"No. Imma talk to him. Alone." Zara started toward the west. Toward the wicked Chad Wilkins. He wouldn't get a third try.

"Zara! Get back here. Don't do anything foolish!"

She paused, looked back over her shoulder, and said, "I'm not the one that tried to burn down the town."

Sheriff Hicks hung his head and reached for her arm. "Zara, it's reckless. You're angry. I'll go."

She searched his face and saw the concern shining in his eyes. She had to be the one to settle the issue with Chad. Sheriff Hicks' bullets wouldn't exorcise the demon inside Chad. Only she had the power to do that, because, well, it wanted her magic, her power. White men always did.

That demon ought to be careful what he asked for.

"So's movin' out to this desert." Zara removed his hand and resumed her trek.

Chad had presented his wickedness.

Now, she'd show him what she had.

As she walked down the path toward the outskirts of town, Zara called upon her ancestors, and one by one, they appeared beside her, dropping out of the sky like falling stars. Each apparition wore his traditional dress of her ancestral homeland. Although some wouldn't consider this a special occasion worthy of the Kente, Zara did. The bright orange and vibrant blue illuminated her surroundings.

Amari

Bwana

Henry

George

Kwame

Soon, the noise of town faded. In the distance coyotes howled, and the light faded. Once she reached Chad's cabin, her ancestors stood with her as watery silhouettes against the velvet night, casting an eerie glow. The two-room home sat on a stretch of barren land. A few feet away, a barn sheltered the beasts, but not the one locked in Chad Wilkins' heart. The light in the window flickered and the sky above sparkled. Zara stood at the end of the walk. The wickedness she'd hope to avoid had provoked this confrontation. Evil. Sinful, the Christians called it.

"I'm callin' you out, Chad Wilkins!"

The door creaked open. A shirtless Chad walked out onto the porch. His bare feet moved silently across the wood. When he saw her, he frowned.

"You survived?"

Her presence answered that, so she didn't reply. She raised her hands as she came closer.

"You always looked lived in, Chad." Zara spied the possessing entity as it hissed out of his mouth, a spiral of buzzing darkness pouring out between his lips toward her. She pulled the wind down and spun her hands to push the attacking evil away and out of sight.

"You oughta died in the fire. Then we'd feast on your power!" Chad screamed, but the voice no longer sounded like him.

"Is Chad still in there?" She'd seen so much death and just plain wickedness. Despite the hard pit of anger in her gut, she wanted Chad to live.

The glowing red eyes narrowed suspecting she meant to trick it. Blisters lined the soles and sides of Chad's feet. He walked as if he felt nothing. The round puss-filled sacks burst with each step, leaving wet tracks behind.

The demon no longer cared for his host.

"Well, is he?"

No reply.

"There's some emptiness that can't be filled, huh?" Zara asked.

Every inch of her hurt. Almost all of her spiritual energy was being syphoned into holding her ancestors here. They helped guide the wind.

"We want you dead!" Chad answered, leaping at her, claws out.

Zara willed the wind once more. Arms heavy with fatigue, she knocked him backwards.

"Power is acquired by taking it," Chad breathed. His descent spiraled down into the absolute wickedness that continued.

"You can't just take what you need. Round here that's called stealin'."

"Not if you're dead," he screamed, stepping down the porch's two flat steps.

"Who'd do the laundry?" Zara wheezed and collapsed to her knees.

So. Weak.

He came at her once more, claws stretched out toward her neck. She pivoted to avoid his right hand, but his sharp nails caught in her left side. They shredded her thin blouse, flesh, and muscle. Chad whirled to face, licking the blood from his fingers.

Gritting her teeth against the searing agony, Zara pushed herself to stand.

He rushed her again, but as he swung, Zara dropped to the dirt. Standing took too much physical strength, of which she had little left. Zara fought to keep her eyes open. She wouldn't cower from death.

"Wait. Who them with you?" Chad squinted, peering with red eyes into the distance.

Zara's ancestors moved to intercept him, and once he spied them up close, he screamed. Turning to run, he tripped and fell, his legs tangled up in each other. Scrambling to his feet, he tried to flee.

Zara's ancestors stepped into her, each one adding their strength of spirit into her body. One after the other, until Zara could stand on her own, full of strong magic and powerful, they joined her. Pain vanished beneath the strength of her ancestors. With them came the iron will to survive the Middle Passage, long lashes of whips, war, and torture.

"No! More!" Zara shouted in the voice of many. With fingers sprayed, she called the winds. They rushed Chad Wilkins, pinning him to the ground. She shortened the distance between them. Once she reached him, she demanded, "Leave Chad. Leave him now! Get out!"

"No!" the demon spat back, laughing in glee. "Kill him. We will still live."

Anger pushed forward, but Zara's ancestors soothed her. *Be calm. We will force him out.*

She pushed the wind, faster. If the demon wanted to stay, it would have to stay in a wind-swept and battered host. Chad screamed until he became unconscious. Before her, the orange glow spiraled out of Chad's body. A mouth split from the entity's mass.

Exhausted, Zara stumbled as her ancestors took their leave, as did her magic. She'd emptied it all.

"Until next time..." the thing promised before slithering into the ground and disappearing from sight.

With her entire being singing in misery, she watched the spot for a moment to make sure the demon didn't crawl back into Chad. With her power temporarily spent, she couldn't protect him.

After a few minutes, Chad stirred awake, his face ripped raw by the wind, his clothes tattered. He glared at her with confusion that melted away to anger.

"You did this to me!"

She nodded, too tired and too hurt to say much more.

"We ain't even, bitch." He coughed and tried to push himself to a sitting position. He collapsed backward with a *thud.*

Zara studied him for a moment, before turning back to the walk. Slowly, she headed down the long path to her home.

————

"Come." Zara sat in front of her fire, a pipe stuck between her teeth, gazing out across the dawn of a new day.

Sheriff Hicks stood in the doorway. "Mornin' Zara. I'm

here about Chad Wilkins. I went over to arrest him this morning, and well, he's in a bad way. Had to call out for the doctor from Tohatchi to come and take a look at 'em."

Zara nodded. Puffed.

Sheriff Hicks shifted his weight to his other foot. "It's lookin' like a heart attack."

"Too much wickedness ain't good for you." Zara met the sheriff's gaze before turning back to the view.

"Yeah?"

"Yeah."

She puffed.

"Funny thing. You went tarrin' after him," Sherriff Hicks said.

Zara puffed. "Imma uneducated person, Sheriff, but I didn't think talkin' to a person could cause them to have a heart attack."

Sherriff Hicks nodded. "It can't."

"All I did was talk to 'em."

He studied her for a few long seconds, before asking, "You comin' in to do the laundry? John said you can set up in one of them back rooms until repairs are done."

"Sure. 'Verybody deserves clean laundry."

The End

THE PLUVIOPHILE

Pluviophile-- lover of rain; someone who finds joy and peace
of mind during rainy days.

Dirt and debris littered the baked asphalt as Interstate
40 cradled empty cars that shimmered in the harsh,
high sunlight. Simone Carter searched the abandoned
highway through the adobe's cracked and sullied screen
window. Eddies skipped along cracked concrete and spun in
dizzying array like quarreling lovers. Forgotten skyscrapers,
apartment buildings, and progress faded from the scorching
sun's brutal, decade-long assault. Death spread across the
land, even as far as the suburbs of Rio Rancho, bleaching
everything with it.

Almost everything. Simone hoped for the discovery of a
pluviophile. As her momma used to say, hope hurt.

"When you get old, like me, you become invisible." Elise mumbled to Simone, drawing her back from her musings and away from the dancing whirls of sand blowing about the streets.

Elise's weathered skin crinkled like leather when she smiled. Gray hair streaked like lightening in a dark sky, her mass of ebony hair. Even inside, the elder woman wore boxy sunglasses over her glasses. The sun's glare shone from car windows and reflected like beacons from their mirrors.

"You ain't invisible, Miss Elise. If you were, I wouldn't bring you the water. I wouldn't waste it." Simone squeezed the elder woman's shoulder, feeling her skinny bones beneath the frail blouse. "Oh, and like always, Spyder said to use it like it ain't gonna last."

Miss Elise stood at the edge of the once revolving door and nodded. Forever stuck by the baked grit and grime, the door led into a once thriving office building. Now, only a few people populated the one-story abode building. Vegetation and animals sought shelter and found solace there. Nature began to retake the remnants of civilization, propelled in desperation by the last trickles of water. Their roots traveled farther and deeper so that they may live. Plowing deep into the cracked upper layers to the moisture buried below.

Simone heard all these things about old age before. She put down the two vats of water onto Elise's porch, and picked up what was left of her patience. The blazing heat fried her nerves and usually turned patience to ash. The wind had gone still. Only the arid heat remained. The water deliveries came at night, but lately Thirsters had been pillaging this section of town. So Simone had come to bring Elise's allotment earlier.

Elise gave her a wide-toothed grin. It sagged at the

corners, like it had been weighed down by life—as if it had withered.

"Life ain't gonna last either. When you get old, you feel death, stalkin' you. Breathin' on your neck. Just like this damn sun. Hot and unrelenting."

"Miss Elise…" Simone paused as she tied a rag over her mouth and nose to keep the dust from getting in. She lowered her goggles, securing them in place across her eyes.

"Blood and bone. That's all that counts in the end." Elise shuffled across the dusty floor. Her slippers scuffed up little tuffs of dirt.

"We're here, now, ain't we? *Alive.* More than bones. More than blood." Simone rested her hands on her hips. She. Elise. Spyder and many others belonged to a community. A grouping of people who decided to live in harmony with nature and pool their resources rather than fight and kill each other. They labored to find water.

"You are such a tender stalk. All of what? Twenty?" Elise shrugged bony shoulders.

She gave Simone the once-over, square oversized sunglasses rose and lowered. Simone tried not to shiver at the seriousness in the elder woman's face. Miss Elise was Navajo, Diné, and she knew things. Rooted into the very fabric of the New Mexican lore and land, the Diné's medicine men and knowledge had been passed down from one mouth to the other. Sometimes Miss Elise saw right through to a person's heart.

With a trembling hand, Miss Elise tossed a silver braid over her thin shoulder. The threadbare blouse contained rose print turned to roseate pink by the sun's bleaching. She eased herself into a rocking chair. Its creaking soon filled the quiet.

"Don't Miss Elise! Don't cry. You wastin' water." Simone

wiped the older woman's cheek with the back of her hand. "Come on, now."

Elise snorted out what sounded like a giggle. "Silly girl." Then with a small smile, she added, "Let me get you some beans."

She got up, knees creaking, and disappeared into the office's breakroom, now turned kitchen. "I've got noisy knees. We elders have broken bodies, Simmie."

Simone pulled her satchel around to her front, where she could open the flap. Beans. Again. Not that she wasn't thankful. But beans grown in cups became tough, small, and tasteless. Simone would eat them anyway. Hunger served as the best spice.

If only the rains would come, they would settle down the rampant dirt and sand blowing about. The wind seemed to enjoy throwing it at people. It howled as folks coughed and wheezed in its storm. The clay flats and sandy riverbeds would be full of cool water. Simone looked to the clear, blue sky. No clouds. No rain. When the wind stopped, the air rippled in waves of heat.

The pluviophiles could call down the rain with their devotion and spells and return everything back to normal. If only she could find one.

"'Ere you go." Elise shuffled out of the building with a glass container a third full with beans. Her dark knowing eyes widened. She beamed, her body blushed in pleasure. "Thank you."

"Thanks. Come over to the Hub later." Simone took the beans, placed them in the satchel and gave Elise a reassuring kiss on the cheek before turning away.

She went down the stairs and onto the sidewalk. A gecko scurried across the parched pavement. The crumbling dust puffed out in her footsteps. The cracked sidewalk led to other parts of the now abandoned Albuquerque neighborhood. Simone walked with quick steps and stopped in shade to avoid the blistering sun. She wore light linen clothes and loose-fitting pants. Motorcycle gloves protected her hands from the bucket's handles cutting into her skin. The goggles kept the dust and sand out of her eyes.

The elders like Miss Elise remembered a time when it had rained, and she envied them. Simone thought she could remember seeing a storm when she was little, but memory and suggestion had melted into *her* truth. Her momma spoke of the time the sky became vengeful. Before the climate changed. The very thing people and animals needed to breathe, *plants*-a staple of the food chain, became scarce. Now, machines pumped out artificial oxygen. Simone hated the aftertaste. Science had explanations for why the rain hadn't come. So did religion. Hell, even the cats had explanations.

No one had solutions.

Ahead, a man dressed in a blinding white suit, dusty sneakers, and beret approached. He stepped out of the shadows and onto the sidewalk as if arriving from the ether. When he removed his hat, a cascade of dreadlocks crashed to his shoulders. He swept them from his face. He replaced the hat with a sigh, and stuck out his hand toward her.

A flicker of recognition and a memory of warning pinged in her brain.

"Simone."

"Rizzo." The surprise in her voice made it sound tighter.

"Haven't seen you in a while." He slipped his hand into his pocket.

"That's by design." Simone held her bag flat against her torso and stepped backward. She didn't know if it was his real name, so few people existed now. That didn't mean you could trust them. He walked slowly as if the sun's heat didn't faze him. Wild eyes seemed to be focused on everything and nothing at once.

Simone wondered if he was *thirsty*.

Or just desperate?

Either made him extremely dangerous. Thirsters had predictable habits and needs. Desperate people didn't have any such thing—only a ravaging madness to kill anyone in their path to water. Some even drank blood to slack their thirst, hence their moniker.

Which was Rizzo?

"The sun is a bitch today." He looked down on Simone as if she had been a lump of meat, festering in the smoldering hot weather.

"Yeah." Simone turned away, anxious to get out of the heat and away from him.

Already sweating, she didn't want to waste another minute outside. She didn't want anything to do with it whatever loony business Rizzo had up his sleeve. If she stayed out too long, the truth would be burned right outta her. That's what her grandmomma used to say.

"Simone! Whoa! Now hold up a minute, sugah."

"Not interested, Rizzo." She rubbed her close-cropped hair. Her scalp itched from the sweat.

"I know how you can get aqua." He shouted. His voice held a hint of panic.

"Buzz off." Simone had heard it all before. Worst pick-up line ever.

At this he grinned. "I'm good for it, Simone."

"Pride cometh before the fall," Simone advised and turned to look at him. She stopped beneath one of the tattered awnings, and puffed out her exhaustion. She tried not to inhale too much of the hot air. Rizzo followed, but stayed one awning behind her.

His smile wilted a bit as his angry eyes met hers.

Touch a nerve, did I?

"I'm serious. I found a pluviophile."

Simone froze. He couldn't have. No one had seen a pluviophile since the rain stopped. They'd become invisible, vanishing just as the world needed them. She frowned. Rizzo had been known for being all show and no substance. But sometimes rumors held nuggets of truth.

"Those don't exist," Simone managed around her dry throat. Great. Cotton mouth.

She removed her bottle from her satchel and took a small sip, barely enough to wet her throat. At this time of day, she couldn't risk drinking more. Overhead a bird cawed. A raven sat perched on an abandoned bus stop sign. They all looked on at her bottle of water with thirsty, dark eyes.

Rizzo smirked. "For real. Honest."

"Honesty can be as big a smoke screen as deceit."

His smirk dissolved. With nothing further, she started off again, resting in the shady spots as she made her way home. When she stopped to catch her breath and to cool off, she took a moment to look back over her shoulder.

Rizzo had gone.

Relief washed over her. A tango with the insane never amounted to anything good or profitable. She didn't think him stupid or incapable. Just strange.

Still. A pluviophile.

It could be true. Simone set off again. Her faith and hope in people, especially those like Rizzo, had dried beneath the unforgiving sun a long time ago.

Shriveled up, like a raisin in the sun.

―――――――

The full moon illuminated the barren land beneath the velvety dark. Laughter and music wafted through the air as evening arrived, and with it, cooler temperatures. Holed up in an abandoned ice cream shop, Spyder's home held round, bistro-style tables, chairs, and a jukebox. Affectionately called The Hub, the row of now vacant homes and businesses along the stretch of retail stores a few blocks from Coronado Mall. Inside, they took advantage of the cooler temperatures. Candles licked at the air, burning bright in the gathering dark. Along the floor sleeping bags lay bunched up in corners and alcoves created beneath tables. It was much cooler outside, with the wind and the breezes. No one camped out there. Too dangerous. At least The Hub's doors locked from the inside. The freezer kept water cold and meat from spoiling.

The drought caused civilization to fall like dominos. Some of the electricity failed when the hydro dam shut down. An outbreak of disease ran rampant due to the lack of sanitation. The world fell because rain wouldn't.

They struggled to find water in dividing lines of a large rock outcrop and at mountain's base.

From one of the corners, Spyder, the de facto leader of their community, grunted and pushed his glasses up the bridge of his nose. Dark green eyes found Simone just as she pushed her goggles into her hair. With his mouth a slash, he crossed his arms across his worn tee shirt. Despite the small quantities of food, Spyder's lean and muscular arms and calloused hands spoke to his work ethic.

"Bullshit. This ain't some old movie. Ain't no saviors, no

more. The only water we got is what we find. What we keep, and what we recycle," Spyder said.

The hushed murmurs stopped.

"What if Rizzo has found a pluviophile?" A chill raced up Simone's spine. She put her hands on her wide hips and fixed her mind to engage with Spyder.

"Chilly?" Spyder quirked an eyebrow. He closed the distance between them, his voice softening as she did so.

"Only on the inside," Simone said.

He frowned and pulled her gently into his embrace. She stiffened in his arms, a wall of annoyance. He wasn't going to charm his way out of this conversation. "Spyder, we can't ignore this. He can take us to one."

Spyder's mouth froze at the corners. "Drink."

He handed her his canteen. He glistened with a sheen of sweat on his face and it pebbled across his upper lip. Simone accepted his peace offering with a small nod.

"Jesus had to distill the water they dug out of that hole over by that shopping mall."

Elise groaned as if a great swollen grief had welled up inside her. She had joined them, and she snorted. "Easy, Spyder. Simone's chasing the rain. My gran used to call it that. When folks believed in them rain people. Some people grow out of that foolishness when they get older, but others get it stuck as truth. It's only myths. Desert fever."

Simone scowled. "I ain't lost in some fairy tale, Miss Elise. A pluviophile had knowledge of the rain, how to make it come, 'cause they loved it. It's because they died out that the rains stopped."

Spyder rolled his eyes. "Rizzo wanna tuck and roll with you, Simmie. He wanna use you to put out his carnal fire. It's a game."

Elise coughed out a chuckle. "Spyder!"

Spyder hugged her close. "It's the sort of thing men tell women."

Simone had thought the same thing, but the more she turned the words over in her mind, the less sure she became. Part of her childhood faith lay in the roots of her need to find the pluviophile not just for herself but for all. They needed water. The daily search for ground water consumed so much of them physically and emotionally. Leaving them as barren as the land.

"The water isn't going to last forever. We got to find another source." Simone tried a different line of discussion. Beneath Spyder's hardened exterior was a man who cared deeply about them.

Spyder's chestnut brown afro caught the candle's soft light. He rubbed his face. She saw the muscle in his cheek throbbing with annoyance. The others had all huddled inside. The murmurs of conversations resumed. Some sat on the floor, others in chairs. A breeze slipped in between the parted doors and tickled the candles' flames. A few open windows helped cool the parlor down. Simone bit her lip to keep from pushing the topic further. She didn't want to cause panic, but their secret place for gathering water didn't replenish itself. The Rio Grande, now known as the Rio Sand, had dried up and the wells around the area had become bone dry. In the last few weeks, they had to go farther out to find pools of water, then boil it, and save it. They dug around for groundwater. Thirsters had to guard to keep others from finding it and taking it, often by violence.

"Yeah, but a person obsessed with rain ain't gonna give us water." Spyder marched away from her and out of the room, toward the back where they used to keep a small desk and office supplies. He used it like a makeshift bedroom.

She followed. An oil lantern cast an oval arc out from the

room's center. Spyder sat down, and clutched a sleeve of water. When he drained it, he released an audible *ah*. He fixed her with a glint in his eyes. He closed the door behind them.

"You can't hide in here, you know. They gonna want answers," Simone whispered, jerking her finger toward the door. "It feels like we're alone in the world."

"We ain't. They frightened of shadows, Simmie. Stop encouraging it." Spyder removed his shirt. Almost as if to take the sting out of his words, he held his hands out to her, palms up. "Come 'ere."

When she placed her hand in his, she smiled. Despite calluses and grit, Spyder's hands made her feel comforted. Being with the group functioned like a human equivalent of a security blanket. She liked being with the others, but Spyder made it all come home. He made her feel wanted, protected and above all—quenched. Their party swelled or dwindled as the months became years, but Spyder remained. An oasis in the desert of her life.

He pulled her into his arms, kissing her cheek. He smelled of earth, mud, and sweat. Those scents all wrapped around his hardened muscles and lean physique. He labored like they all did, but not just for himself, for *all* of them. A trait she admired. He led with one solitary focus. *Stay alive.*

"You cloudin' the issue." *Stay focused on the topic at hand.* Simone tried to stop the smile from emerging on her face.

"Yeah, I am," he breathed, voice heady with longing, eyes smoky with desire.

Simone giggled at the brush of his new growth against her skin. Her heart swelled when his lips focused on the soft hallow of her neck.

"Your only concern is for satisfyin' your appetite." Simone hated the words sounded so breathless.

He crumpled to the sleeping bed. He glowered at her. "I'll

satisfy yours, too." His verdant-colored eyes seemed lush in the low light. His lips parted and he looked thirsty. Simone figured he hungered for something other than food and drink.

Simone's voice stalled out.

When his lips covered hers, she dissolved into the hot yearning unwinding in her.

All thoughts of rain dried up beneath the flames of desire.

———

B right overhead sky showered sunlight down on the leftover remnants of the city. No humidity. Only the endless knitting of sweltering days bleeding into each other. Simone's straw hat kept it from blinding her. The goggles helped too, but cloud coverage would be better. Rain would be a blessing. She searched for leafy plants. They indicated a water source the plants need for those big leafy greens. The demise of native grasses meant cattle starved until they died out. A few goats provided milk and meat. The Chihuahuan Desert expanded. The biodiversity declined. Soon the landscape, water failed to recharge the crucial aquifers and overflow pools.

The suburbs and the desert collided. The desert won. Without vegetation to hold the soil in place, sand and dust blew freely in the winds.

The hike to the abandoned home improvement store took longer than usual. Someone had burned out three or four cars in the night. The lingering scent of sulfur and fire hung in the atmosphere. Billowing black smoke pushed into the hot air.

The barrels sat rejected, just off the street, causing a large bonfire. With everything so dry, the flames raged on without extinguishing. No one would waste the water to put it out.

After three miles, she reached the blue oval barrels lined in rows in the store's garden section. Hidden beneath a gray, weather-worn tarp, and beneath a shady location. The barrels sat like chubby children cowering from the squall. One that would never come. If the rain would fall and fill the barrels' bellies, all would be well. The world could heal. She longed to frolic in the falling droplets. To feel them go splat against her skin. Feel the water glide down her back.

Instead, she was here to replenish the dregs of her water supply.

Simone held her waterskins beneath the spout of one of the water barrels. The lip of the water bladder held on tight as the liquid coursed into it. Quiet gurgling made her smile. When the water skin had filled, she capped it and slung it over her chest, along with her satchel.

Earlier in the morning, Spyder, with half of their group members, had left to go scout for water. That singular task consumed all of his waking moments. *Get water.*

She had other plans. Last night, once Spyder fell asleep, she'd lain awake, staring at the flickering of the oil lamp's flame. Now that Rizzo had presented the possibility, she couldn't stop thinking about finding a pluviophile. Now, she decided she had to at least meet the person—or try. If it were true, it could change everything. For one, it would bring back the bees. Honey. Sweetness. The heavens knew her bitter life could use a little honey. Rain would bring it all back.

"Bees are very sensitive. They're prone to stress," Simone advised the chain link fence as she crawled through a pulled back section and out into the parking lot. Weak vegetation clung to life in decrepit and crumbling pots. Faded paint parking lines held spots for memories and phantoms.

Something stirred in her spine.

"How are bees in a storm?" Rizzo called from behind, spooking her.

She spun around. "Rizzo?"

"Lost. The winged insects would be lost in a storm." He laughed as he spilled out of a van. It didn't have wheels, but it rested on blocks. The windows had been burst out and the passenger slide-rear door sat open.

Curtains caught the breeze and fluttered out of the open door. Dressed again in dingy slacks and a gray tee shirt, he seemed very clean. How? When no one dared spare the water to clean clothes? To wash bodies except to sponge office. Perhaps he did know a pluvophile. His sun-kissed dreadlocks had been tied behind him, low at the base of his neck, with a red-faded bandana. Rizzo still had that restlessness of the body that gave her pause.

She'd never seen anyone so close to their aqua supply. Did he know about their stash? Had he been using it? Sharing their resources, unbeknownst to them?

Simone swallowed hard and stepped further away from their stash and from Rizzo. Fighting the urge to look back at the hidden barrels, she put the location to her back and started toward the house area. At some point, she'd make a right and circle back to The Hub. Was he stalking her?

Rizzo fell in step beside her. "I figured you'd come to me sooner or later."

"Who says I was comin' to you?" She adjusted the satchel, but slowed her pace. They'd reached the corner, the barrels out of sight. She lowered her googles and raised the bandana over her mouth.

Already, the sun slipped out from behind a perfect, white

puffy cloud. No signs of rain. No surprise. They stepped down from the sidewalk and out onto the street. Nothing moved. Sterile still.

"Elise said you'd probably come 'round today." He grinned at that knowledge.

She stopped. So maybe the old woman wasn't one sandwich short of a picnic. On the other hand, Rizzo could be lying his pants off. "You ain't gonna be messin' with Miss Elise."

Rizzo chuckled, but it made Simone's skin crawl. "No. I had gone across her area, uh, lookin' for somethin' and she had been sittin' on her porch. Sippin'."

"You were over in The Hub." She quirked an eyebrow at Rizzo. Perhaps he *was* stalking her. Rizzo didn't hang around them. Rizzo reminded her of hyenas, scavenging around the parched land, waiting for a chance to take from others.

He wouldn't meet her eyes and his smile had gone. The faraway expression on his face changed. He spoke soft against the wind.

"Yeah. You see, she talked about the time before, when the August rains would come. The smell of wet earth and delicious droplets splattering against her face. The way it whipped through the wind and drenched her hair, pooled in her ears, and slipped seductively down her collar. Then she remembered the tight panic when people started realizin' they wouldn't feel the rain again. That Elise remembers at all is amazin'."

"I think Miss Elise remembers, so we can't forget." Simone started away from him. The woman held loads of stories about the time before, when life breathed at the splash of rain. When lush gardens grew with abandon and fed everyone—people, animal, and insects alike.

Rizzo nodded. He smiled. Unlike his others, this one seemed to sprout from a real emotion. She just wasn't sure which feeling it was.

"So, um, you wanna see her?" He looked out toward the Sandia Mountains.

Simone sighed. "You know, I'm with Spyder."

"Yeah. I know. This ain't about him. You a *believer*."

"You don't know me."

Rizzo inclined his head. "No, but your kind. I see the way you always searchin' the sky for the elusive gray clouds."

Simone swallowed to ease the dryness in her throat.

She shifted her satchel, more to give her hands something to do than any real discomfort. Already the day inched toward white-hot. Her shirt stuck to her back. She didn't want to be out any longer than she had to be, especially with Rizzo.

"Tell me true. Do you really know one?" Simone asked.

Rizzo flashed teeth before nodding. "Come on."

Simone's stomach tightened as the thrill shot through her. She hesitated, but only just.

"Is it far?" She couldn't waste the water for a wild goose chase.

"No."

"We should wait for the evening, when it's cooler."

He shook his head. "We go now or never."

"Never." Simone called his bluff. Why the rush? No one travels during the hottest part of the day.

"Are you sure you won't come?" Rizzo closed the van's door and set off north, away from downtown and toward Santa Fe.

Simone waited a few moments, before she followed.

In the many years she'd lived on The Hub, she'd never

ventured further than about ten miles surrounding the area. What if he meant to take her to those undesirable parts of the city Miss Elise and a few of the other old people warned of? Graffiti sprayed across bridges and walls warned of trespassers, strangers, and scavengers. *Thirsters.* They stole people and sold them to people who ate them and drank their blood.

They should push on at night to avoid the burning heat of day. The perils and dangers of the night faded during the day, but the daylight had its own hazards. Simone didn't want to be alone with Rizzo. Something itched at the back of her consciousness about him. Despite that, the eagerness to see an actual pluviophile shoved all doubts to the edge of caution.

"I can tell you don't believe me." Rizzo's serious profile made him seem stern, but his voice held amusement.

"It ain't that, but nobody's seen a pluviophile in a long time." Simone confessed.

He nodded and stopped. He cupped his hands around his mouth. "There's reason for that. Can't just have people fawning all over them and tryin' them."

"Tryin' *them*? There's more than one?" Her heart skipped a beat. *Could it be really true?*

"Yeah. Pluviophiles, well, they love the rain."

Simone didn't move, but folded her arms across her chest. "If there's so many why don't they make rain? They have the knowledge. Their devotion to it should make it start again. People are dying!"

Rizzo's lips twitched like he wanted to say something, but he didn't. Instead, he started walking again, and Simone joined him with her fear ebbing away, eroding her hope. The entire endeavor seemed like a walk across a tight rope—one minute she felt safe, comfortable on the thin stretch of Rizzo's claim. The other she felt like she'd tip over and plunge to her death.

She checked her satchel and water. "So, it's not far."

They walked for a long time. Simone watched the building structures dissolve into greater eroded states, and the occasional covered person scurrying out of the sun's constant assault—vanishing and reappearing. She sipped from her waterskin often, but Rizzo never took a drink. After they'd walked about four miles, they stopped at an abandoned restaurant. The building's rustic exterior bore a cowboy theme. It seemed perfect in the dirt and dust and tumbleweeds. Rizzo opened the door and went into its darkened seating area. He moved with familiarity to the back, to the kitchen. Simone stepped with caution. Her stomach grumbled with hunger.

When Rizzo reappeared, he carried a lit lantern and a small bowl of fruit. He placed them on a table and beckoned her to join him. *Fruit.* She hadn't seen the like of fruit in, well, in a long time.

"Takes water to grow them." She picked up a small plum.

Rizzo nodded as he bit into one. It gushed its juiciness. He wiped the liquid from his mouth with the back of his hand. "Time. Water. Yeah. I have a source outside of Socorro and Las Cruces that had cacti when the rain stopped. They use it sparingly to cultivate plants. Food. Fruit. They also used other sources. Shrubs ain't good for nutrients. Black Gramma took up a lot of the area, but now just sparse sections of what used to be lawns."

"How far are we from The Hub?" Simone asked. The plum's smooth skin felt foreign, strange in her palm.

"Dunno. About five or six miles, maybe more."

"Where are we goin'?"

"I told you."

"Yeah, but *where* are we goin' for real? What place?"

Simone bit into the plum and it tasted sweet, juicy. Unprepared for its juiciness, it spilled down the corner of her mouth. She'd never tasted anything as delicious as this! Her childhood came rushing back with the gush of sweetness. Lazy days of summer rain and the rich aroma of wet earth filled her senses.

Rizzo hadn't really told her anything, but she rolled the plum around in her palm.

"So, where does this person reside? Why haven't they returned the rains?"

Rizzo bit into another plum. "There must be believers, Simone. No one wants to waste their power on the unappreciative. That's why we're in this mess. We aren't worthy of saving."

A shadow fell across the restaurant's entranceway.

"There you are." Spyder's voice held relief before the hot rise of anger changed his tone. "I was delayed."

Simone nodded, thankful he arrived at all. Thirsters had taken to drinking blood to feed, their ravenous and constant thirst. An unbearable thought that made Simone groan.

Rizzo bolted to his feet, but he didn't seem surprised. He stalked over to Spyder, reached into his pocket, and pulled out an image. Simone came around to look too. The charred edges looked like he'd pulled it from a fire. In the foreground, a palm covered a face and a mop of ebony curls could be seen. What made Simone catch her breath was behind the person, was what looked like big droplets of rain.

Why hadn't he showed her this before?

"Nothin' like a little bit of truth to sell the biggest lie," Spyder remarked as he took the photo from Rizzo. "You drag her out here on a damn wild goose chase. Wastin' her water supply and mine."

Rizzo frowned, and dropped back a step. "You didn't have to follow."

"Who is it?" Simone cut through the male squabble, and took the photo from Spyder for a closer look.

"I promised not to say." Rizzo shoved his hands into his pockets. Now, he looked as shifty as Spyder had said.

"Why tell me, Rizzo, that you found one and drag me out here? What are you playin' at?" Simone snatched up her satchel. "Damn you."

"I thought you wanted to see her." Rizzo grabbed the photo and put it away, avoiding her eyes.

"Come, Simmie." Spyder waved his hand to the open door. "Fun's over."

Sunlight barged in and for a moment, she didn't want to push on again through the blaze. Simone swore. She'd come all this way just to be outdone by Rizzo. At this rate, she'd never get to meet a real pluviophile.

"We should wait until dusk." Simone sighed.

Spyder paused. He searched her face. "Yes, but let's get someplace safe."

Rizzo interjected. "I can show you, Simone. You're a believer. Your faith glows."

He came to her and met her unflinching gaze.

Spyder swore. "You gonna believe him and his mumbo jumbo?"

"I wanna make up my own mind, not have it done for me." She shot back.

Spyder adjusted his backpack. He held her gaze as if contemplating the seriousness of her words. Something in her face must have convinced him.

"I ain't leavin' you. No, not while I still draw breath." Spyder's scowl could burn down whole cities, but it was all for Rizzo.

She smiled. Beneath his anger and quick dismissiveness, Spyder held something tender deep inside. Theirs was a tough life. Spyder had to be hard on the outside, but underneath lay a sensitive and loving man.

Rizzo looked from her to Spyder and then back again. "We wait for dark."

———

Once the skyline blushed and the hint of twilight flirted around the edges of the day, the three of them started again. The nocturnal sounds of insects and small lizards scurrying in the dark became a background music for Simone. Spyder and Rizzo carried flashlights, but she carried a lit oil lantern. Fresh batteries were hard to come by, but Spyder had managed to get some renewable ones. He charged them at The Hub for the flashlights.

In the low light, Simone had lost track of the direction they'd come. The mountains seemed closer, but she couldn't be sure. The petroglyphs had been hidden by the falling night. Exhausted, tired, and hot, Simone longed for her sleeping bag alongside Spyder back at The Hub. Right now the others were probably singing songs, laughing, and telling stories of the old days when the rain drenched the world in wet, sloppy kisses.

At last, they reached what once had been a residential area. Homes crumbled along the road. Little else had remained intact. Simone reached a utility pole and slumped against it. Rizzo stopped and looked over his shoulder.

Spyder had come to a stop beside Simone, but he didn't reach for the strength of the pole. His mouth was a slash of annoyance.

"We go no further." Spyder crossed his arms.

"There's not much farther to go," Rizzo replied, his tone flat.

"You said that the last five miles. Where is it?" Simone wiped her forehead.

"Next block." Rizzo gestured to the buildings in the distance before turning and walking off.

"We're goin' back." Spyder stalked over to Simone, giving her his don't argue face.

Rizzo stepped into the other man's personal space. "She always looks at you like her soul is swimming in your wake, Spyder. Does it really scare you that I mean to give her something you can't? Help her with her faith. Show her the way to our salvation."

"Like you could. Any natural mimic could pretend to be a pluviophile," Spyder accused. "Toss some water on the person. Take the picture. False hope to folks with faith. You're pathetic."

"I wouldn't waste the water for a joke!" Rizzo shouted back.

"But you would to pull her into your web." Spyder smirked at Rizzo, and it looked ugly on his face.

Simone stared at Rizzo in disbelief. Had all of this been a ruse to get her alone with him? It seemed ridiculous, but Spyder's words had wormed into her doubts and amplified them.

"You created this ruse, Rizzo?" Simone pushed herself off the pole.

"Stay away from us." Spyder's hand moved to his blade in its scabbard at his waist. He used it to threaten Thirsters and other scavengers. Guns worked better, and he kept one of those hidden in his ankle holster. He didn't use it often except for hunting. He didn't like wasting ammunition on people.

"I'm tryin' to help, too. Those water barrels are almost dry," Rizzo proclaimed. He looked at Simone. "Simone..."

Spyder jerked Simone around behind him, and glared at Rizzo. "You act like a functioning *thirster*! So focused on her. That's what you're really after..."

With that, Spyder guided Simone over to a shady spot beside a house. Simone shook Spyder off. With her heart smarting, she faced him.

"You ruined it! We're this close to finding a pluviophile." Simone balled her hands into fists.

He shook his head. "There was nothing to ruin. The guy's a liar."

"You don't know that for sure." Simone swallowed the rest of her rant. She couldn't afford to get too excited. She had already lost enough water by sweating.

"The cleverest lies are the ones we're ready to believe, Simmie." He reached for her again. She pulled away.

"I believe..."

"You *want* to believe!" Spyder threw up his hands.

"Yeah! I do! What's wrong with believin' in something'? This life ain't bitter and hard enough but to have nothin' to shoot for? Nothin' to hope?"

Spyder grew still. "This life is what we got. It ain't bad. It ain't great. But it's ours."

She couldn't form words enough to express her feelings, so she glared.

"The guy's a weirdo," Spyder continued, his voice softening, the way it did when he wanted to soothe her.

"Spyder!"

He looked up at her, and she saw the muscle in his jaw work.

Rizzo came over to them. He looked like he had a key. When he caught her eye, she saw disappointment on his face. She'd been too scared to risk going with him further. Spyder's arrival had been a relief, and Simone didn't like the feeling that knowledge left inside of her. She tittered on the edge of decision—to follow her heart and on to the pluviophile or with her gut that warned that nothing Rizzo promised bore weight.

"That's fine. I'd let the fear win. We all did." She adjusted her satchel. "What's the key for?"

"This key is for that." Rizzo nodded a home, pushed back off the curb and down further in the cut. "We're here."

Simone followed his pointed finger to the older adobe dwelling. It sat on a slab of bedrock, cut off from the other homes in the area. Long ago, cattle rustled by cowboys and thieves occupied this space. The iron gate throbbed in the sunlight, and Rizzo gestured to its closed wooden door.

Rizzo came closer to her, seemingly unafraid of Spyder's looming presence. It occurred to her then that the restless warnings she'd felt around Rizzo had been his lack of fear.

"We can go inside," Rizzo said.

Spyder glared at him. "No, we can't."

Simone followed him, her thighs screaming in agony. She couldn't take one more step, but she must. They'd walked further than she'd ever been, to the promised land. Just like the biblical children of Israel wandering around in the desert for 40 years, waiting for God to deem them ready for the promised pluviophile. Was Rizzo some bastardized Moses, funneling her faith and her belief through his own filter?

Somewhere lay the only other person or persons who

could save them. She had to push on. Beside her, Spyder remained silent, his mood increasingly black.

Ahead, Rizzo stopped in front of an adobe home with a peeling scarlet door. He glanced back to make sure they were coming, and then approached with slow, careful movements. Once he reached the door handle, he turned it, and stepped inside. The dark interior seemed to flow out into the night to greet them. He paused, pointed his flashlight into its innards, and then waved them forward.

Spyder cut ahead of her, pushed ahead, and held his arm out, barring Simone's path.

"It's gettin' dark. Send her out," Spyder demanded.

Rizzo shook his head. "That ain't how it works." He shifted his gaze to Simone. "You came a long way."

Simone stepped around Spyder's outstretched arm. "Let me see her."

"Don't let him goad ya into somethin' stupid, Simmie." Spyder shifted to stop her.

She sidestepped him again, her energy siphoning off, and her waterskin empty. Now. So close. She wouldn't turn tail and go home. Spyder opened his cracked lips to argue, but he didn't. He merely followed her in. True the last slips of summer days threatened to drop to complete darkness, but they had time.

The odor of something old, moldy and wet hung in the air just as they cleared the threshold. It took a few moments for her eyes to adjust to the dim.

Ahead, Rizzo moved on, moving from memory, lighting lanterns, and candles. The room held chairs, and what looked like pews. She didn't really pay too much attention. Up the winding stairs, Rizzo dipped into the first room on the right. Simone's heartbeat raced.

Finally.

"Come this way." Rizzo stuck his head out over the banister, holding up a lantern, and waving them up.

Now. She'd get to meet those who could bring the rain. The stairs creaked beneath her weight, but she continued with weariness and fatigue sapping her strength. She powered on from sheer will.

Her faith sustained her, for little else could.

S imone entered the room to find seated closest to the window, a frail, elderly woman dressed in a long, ruffled blouse, what looked like a broom skirt, and bare, worn feet. The woman turned, in agonizing slow movements to look at them. A scarf covered a head much too small to hold an adult brain. The big armchair seemed to be at the cusp of swallowing her up, and for just the smallest moment, Simone wondered if this was it. All her great, looming hope had been compacted and conjured into this puff of a person.

"You here to see the pluviophile?" The voice creaked like it hadn't been used in ages. The body moved as if the joints needed oil, lubrication, and prying into the right fit. An empty mouth gaped into a grin devoid of teeth.

"They have come a long way," Rizzo said with a gentle tone.

He seemed to just appear beside the ancient woman, like an apparition. He helped lift the person to her feet, expelling her from the chair. She didn't walk over to them, but rather gestured for Simone to come forward.

Was this it? This is the moment I've waited my entire life to partake.

Simone inched further, disappointment blooming in her stomach, disturbing the butterflies. She felt both sick and angry all balled into a pit, burning in its indignation. Behind her, Spyder remained like a stony sentry—still and waiting.

"Rizzo." Simone heard the sharp annoyance in her tone.

"Simone."

What is this foolishness?

She hadn't come all this way to just do nothing.

The elderly woman took her hand. Chills skated up Simone's arm and she tried to reclaim her hand, but the grip remained surprisingly strong.

"You love the rain?" Her breath felt cold against Simone's fingers. It sounded old, like a once defunct spigot.

"Yes…I do, but…" Simone's heart raced like a stallion in the old videos she used to watch as child. Galloping to flee, thundering in freedom—and fear.

"Then they will come again," the old woman creaked. She offered a toothless smile, and the acidic aroma of her breath.

"How?" Simone whispered, forcing herself not to recoil, not to tear her hand away and flee. "People are still dropping like flies from the droughts. Everything continues to crumble."

"You know how," she cackled, dark eyes sparkling in the low light. "You always known how. It's etched into your memory."

My memory? What does that mean?

"Tell me how you're going to make the rains return." Simone pressed, her throat thick with unshed tears. She'd not waste the water, but damn it, she had to know. "You're a pluviophile. You must know how to bring them back."

The elderly woman gave her yet another opened mouth grin, full of emptiness, and bad breath. Like her mouth, the world had become a wasteland of death, struggle, and famine. This was no pluviophile.

Simone jerked her hand free. "This is bullshit." With her

heart hammering, she whirled around to Rizzo. "You dragged me out here for this? A heart to heart with your grandmother?"

Rizzo balked. "She's not my grandmother."

"I love the rain. Its strong aroma, and its life-bringing water," the woman interjected with glassy eyes. She reached out as if she could touch those wet drops. "I love it so much, we offer sacrifices to the gods to help them return."

Gripped in silent terror, Simone whispered. "What?"

With her anger crumbling, Simone looked back for Spyder, just as Rizzo leapt forward and tried to grab her.

"Don't touch me!" Simone shouted and twisted out of his grasp.

"Come back here!" Rizzo roared.

Simone's vision narrowed. Rizzo had something shiny in his hands. A burning sensation flared along her forearm, where he grabbed her. An angry, but tiny dot showed she'd been stabbed. But with what? She stumbled and her hand shot for stability. A tingling took up residence in Simone's ears and she spun to Spyder. Tittering, she tripped over something small and fuzzy and crashed to the floor.

"Spyder!" It sounded as if it came from far away.

The elderly woman shook with laughter. "Excellent job, Rizzo. Excellent. Another one for the rains."

"What's goin' on? What did. You. Do?" The words came from her lips, but Rizzo, Spyder, and the elder woman smeared across her vision. "Spyder!"

Darkness ebbed at the edges of Simone's vision, consuming the light, consuming her faith. She'd missed the evil danger.

And yet, at that moment, she could feel splats of water against her face. Impossible, she'd been inside a room, but still the coolness coursed down her neck. Rain didn't fall indoors. Nothing made sense, and as the world slid sideways, Simone heard desperate screaming.

It wouldn't be until later she realized those screams came from her.

———

W et and cool water raced down her face.

The rains. They'd returned! I did it! I found the pluviophile.

With this joy thundering in her heart, Simone's eyes flapped open and she bolted to a sitting position, arms raised to collect the precious rain into her palms and rejoice.

She wasn't outside.

She was in a room. All around her, the space bore the brunt of hard theft and vandalism. Nothing looked familiar, except for the man leaning against the broken windowpane. The sunglasses had been pushed up into his hair, and his grim expression vanished when he met her eyes.

Spyder.

"You awake." Something soft in his voice touched her. He put the cap back on his waterskin, tightening it.

"When you sprinkle on people's face, you gonna wake 'em up." Simone stretched, but her head pounded. She considered lying back down, but then thought better of it. Her mood plummeted. No rains. No pluviophile. "Where are we?"

"At the midpoint between home and that place." Spyder looked away. "You have every right to harbor a grudge against me."

"Why?"

"I stepped out of the room, left you alone with Rizzo and that woman. I should've been there. They almost had you."

Simone tried to access the memory, but a thick fog huddled in her brain blocking her access. "What happened after he drugged me?"

Spyder sighed. "I grabbed you, just as you passed out. Rizzo pulled a knife. We fought. Here we are."

Simone became quiet. How did he manage to get her out of that house? How far did he have to travel to wherever this was? She wanted to know everything that happened since Rizzo rendered her unconscious.

"Where are we?" She asked.

"I dunno. A place to rest until you woke. But now that you are, we've got other problems. We outta water."

"And Rizzo. Is he following us?" Simone got to her feet, using the nearby table to help her get to her feet.

"I don't think so. Rizzo scurried off into the night after I sent him packing," Spyder's voice sounded funny, but he wouldn't come to her, either. He remained standing by the window.

"The pluviophile?"

"A lie." Spyder shifted a little.

"The old woman?" Simone took an unsteady step toward him. Her muscles complained as she did so, as if she'd been asleep for days. Still somewhat hazy, she swayed before gaining balance.

"You must've been more dehydrated than I thought." Spyder came over to her and kissed her forehead. "You don't remember anything, do you?"

"No." She allowed him to embrace her.

"Okay, so you remember the old woman?"

Simone nodded.

"Rizzo lied to you. They weren't pluvophiles. They were hunting people to sacrifice to the gods to make the rains return. They probably would've cut off your juicy bits and then sacrificed you."

"No." Simone broke Spyder's embrace. "No!"

Spyder nodded. "Rizzo tried to get you into his arms, holding your hand, and stuff. Found out he'd laced your waterskin and the fruit you ate. It also looked like, when that didn't work fast enough, he used some needle to inject you with something to knock you out." Spyder held up her forearm. He touched it.

"Ow!" Simone wrenched her arm free. "That hurts."

"Yeah." Spyder laughed, but then his face became serious. "You don't remember any of that? You were unconscious, but I didn't know how deeply."

"That's impossible. How could he put somethin' in it? It was with me the whole time." Simone felt cold. Yet, the reality dawn on her and burned like the unforgiving sun. She had the bruise on her forearm. She did recall her inner voice's warning the alarm that something, or rather, everything was off about the elderly woman, about Rizzo, but her hunger to *believe* had made her risk her safety—and Spyder's.

"Was it?" Spyder tossed another waterskin onto her lap. "Is that one yours?"

Simone fingered the leather. The lines looked familiar, and it was the same color. "Looks like it."

"It ain't. It's mine." Spyder said. "Maybe he meant to drug me. I dunno what his crazy ass was thinking."

"So, no pluviophile?" Simone sighed.

"I dunno, Simmie. There wasn't no pluviophile *there*. He tried to take you. Around these parts some have taken to selling people, women, to run the waterlines, too."

"I know it, but this seemed different." Simone rubbed her face with her hands.

"You wanted it to be different." Spyder reached for her

and tucked her into his embrace. His hot breath brushed her ear as he whispered, "I beat his ass for tryin'."

"Spyder..." Simone felt numb. "Why drag me all this way? Why fake a pluviophile?"

"The man's a predator. He preyed on your faith and your hope. I think my comin' spoiled his plans. He kept walkin' cause he wanted to wear us out, wear us down so we'd be easier to control."

Simone hugged him. With her face laid against his chest, she felt him wince. "Are you all right?"

"Yeah. Small injury." Spyder wheezed.

She stepped back. "What?"

Spyder grimaced and lifted his shirt. A tight cut leaked watery ribbons of blood down his taut abdomen. "I did say I was in a fight."

"Spyder! It's not even closed."

She tore his shirt's edge and began tying a tourniquet across his wound. They had to get back home. Reggie, the local doctor, could stitch him up. Why didn't she trust Spyder and just go back to the way things had always been? Foolish childhood's dream of chasing a damn pluviophile.

"I know that look. Don't fret." Spyder gave her a weak grin. The ends of his mouth trembled.

"It's all my fault." Simone held him close, careful not to squeeze too hard. Her hands were now sticky with blood, but she wouldn't waste the water to clean them, if they had any.

"No, Simmie. It's Rizzo's. Ain't nothing wrong with a little faith. Keep believin'. One day the rains will return."

Simone looked out across the sun, now setting in the west. It painted the heavens in beautiful hues of rose and purples, all representative of the desert, of Albuquerque, and the land she'd been born into it. A harshness existed here, but it had for thousands of years, even with the rains. She'd been foolish to seek after what she now realized to be truth. Her people had survived this environment for ages. And they—she—would do so still.

It didn't take a pluviophile to know that.

The End

RISE

In the distance, Phoenix rose out of the Arizona desert like the mythical bird of legend. Its wings stretched far and wide in brilliant glimmering glass and metal monoliths and skyscrapers. Phenomenal Phoenix promised heavenly homes and a new start. Burn your past life and rise into freedom.

The wind howled as Trixie and Fox yanked their hoods over their heads and stepped onto the gravel road. The truck driver roared by them, spraying apathy and debris. Trixie adjusted her braids into a low ponytail beneath her hood, before hugging Fox to her. Overhead, the mountains reached for the night sky. Decked out in diamond-like stars, the velvety evening heaven had been decorated as if in celebration of their arrival.

"Nobody wants us." Fox shrugged out of her embrace. Already taller, her younger brother teetered in the awkward stage between child and man. Tinged with disappointment, his words pinched her heart.

She hugged him close. "Then we'll have us. You build a

home out of people, not places." Trixie linked her arm through his. Despite the scowl on his face, she saw him grin quickly before allowing it to dissolve again.

"We'll rise from the ashes of our past." Trixie patted him on the back.

"Uh huh. Covered in soot."

A small chapel rose out of the dust. Trixie headed there as the Arizona sky opened up and rain fell hard and fast. Running to the worn wooden door, she and Fox huddled from the raging squall. The tiny archway provided little cover as the rain pelted them.

"Can't you do somethin'?" Fox shouted above the clap of thunder.

Trixie sighed. "It's just a little water!"

"I'm drownin' standin' up!"

Trixie placed her palm against the wood and concentrated. She could feel the molecules accelerate faster. The wood crackled and buckled beneath the fire. She burned through the door enough for her to stick her hand in and unlock it.

"Come on!" She pulled Fox inside.

Mold, dampness, and desert odors collected in the chapel's stuffy air. The pews sat in neat rows. Fox picked up one of the tiny tealight candles and passed it to her. With a snap of her fingers, she lit all three rows of candles, including the one in Fox's hand. Her powers had grown since the Flagstaff forest fires.

"Trix!" he shouted, startled by her actions. He replaced it with the others before turning back to her. "You could've burned me."

She looked back over her shoulder. "No. I've got better control now."

Fox inclined his head, but thankfully did not push the matter. Trixie wiped the ash from her hands and took a look around. The tiny chapel had been deserted. Dust bunnies and layers of sand covered everything. Not that the conditions meant anything. In the desert, dust and sand covered everything, except in Phoenix.

She would dust off the ashes of her past.

"Doesn't look like anyone's been blessed in this place in a while."

"It's a blessing for us, then isn't it?" Trixie picked up a hymn book. Its jacket had been worn down to cardboard inside.

Fox quirked an eyebrow at her. "I guess so."

She paused at the hesitation in his voice. Fox's locks, a bright sun-brushed red, provided evidence of their father's Irish lineage. His dark skin spoke to their momma's deep roots in Africa. Like so many in the after-throes of a collapsed country, the genetics didn't matter—only what they could do with their abilities did.

But not in the land of the sun. All were equal there.

"I know it ain't the best of situations but it's the only place for tonight. Tomorrow…"

"…we see the sun." Fox finished.

She placed the book back on the pew.

Fox tossed his hood back, and his long dreadlocks spilled over his shoulders. His eyes glowed in the evening's gloom. "It ain't gonna be no different there. Nobody wants us. Too dangerous."

Trixie plopped down onto the first pew and conjured fire from her palm. She held it high as she searched around her immediate area. Fatigued, hungry, and crashing from the adrenaline waning in her veins, Trixie couldn't quite put her hands on the right words to ease Fox's fear.

"All are welcomed there. You remember those stories of emancipation we read on the Internet? Of the Israelites out of Egypt? Of the Africans who escaped slavery to the North?"

Closing her eyes, she forced the flames in her hand to recede. Her palm stung, but she didn't bother to check it, not any more. Her hands carried the blackened char of ash. The doctors and scientists couldn't stop that. The tests, the surgeries, and numerous drugs all failed to eradicate it.

A genetic oddity.

Magician.

Freak.

Nigger.

She rolled over onto her side. None of the labels meant anything in Phoenix. Everyone could take flight.

"I bet that place ain't seen nothin' like us." Fox huffed. He kept trying to find some identifier, some *adjective* that would make him fit in to a world obsessed with labelling everything and shoving it into its proper place.

"We *are* dangerous, Fox. And tired. Well, I am." Trixie stretched out on the pew and folded her hands behind her head. Her thick frame didn't fit entirely on the narrow wood, but she made it work. Her hoodie served as an adequate pillow.

"Maybe we wouldn't be dangerous, if they hadn't kept us like animals in that—that place," Fox said.

The pew behind her creaked beneath Fox's weight. Books, no doubt the hymnals, hit the floor with a series of *thuds*.

"Fox…"

"All right. Lettin' go, sis."

She smiled. "Goodnight, Red."

"I'm a man, not a color."

She giggled as sleep approached. His complaints at her teasing meant Fox hadn't lost all of his innocence and youth—yet.

———

The *smack* of the chair forced Trixie to jump awake with a shriek. Startled from her slumber, she fell with a crash to the floor. Worn and frayed carpet had muffled some of the sound, but Trixie had been spooked. With her elbow smarting, and a full-on grimace, she got to her feet.

What the hell?

They weren't alone. She stood with her hands aflame and her temper even hotter. "Who are you?"

A large man dressed in a black robe stood across from her. White-blonde shoulder-length hair and cold azure eyes loomed beneath the cloak's hood.

"Hello?" Trixie stepped in front of the pew where Fox had just sat up.

"Trix?" Fox yawned from behind her.

"Who are you?" Trixie positioned her hands.

She took in everything in flashes. The brightness of the chapel. The silence of the people. The scent of something *other* in the air. The hush from outside. Last night, the chapel had been abandoned. No signs of life at all, but then—in her exhaustion, and in the gathering dark—she could have miscalculated.

"Hey! She's talkin' to you!" Fox pulled himself up to his full height.

The man in the robe faced them. He threw back the cloak's hood, and nodded in Fox's direction. "You aren't headed for the sun, are you?"

"Who are you again?"

"The sun is a funny thing. It attracts with its beauty and warmth. It also kills with those same qualities."

When he spoke, it thundered, like a powerful waterfall.

The hairs on her neck rose at the man's sheer power. Fear gnawed at the edge of Trixie's courage. What was he?

"Oy, we asked ya first." Fox's glowing eyes shifted to her and then back to the man.

Trixie lowered her hands and mentally extinguished their fire. If this escalated, Fox could get hurt.

"I'm sorry. We trespassed on your property." Trixie picked up her pack.

The man nodded again. "Apology accepted."

"We didn't see no sign. Nothin'." Fox added.

The leader in the cloak had taken several small steps toward them but halted at Fox's words.

"So, uh, who are you?" Trixie asked. She adjusted her hoodie as she walked closer to Fox. If they had to make a run for it or fight their way out, she wanted to be within arm's reach of him.

She wouldn't let anything come between her and freedom. To be her true self. She'd rise above.

"My name is of no importance. What I *do*, now, Trixie and Fox, is what matters most."

"How do you know our names?" Trixie took several steps back.

The man flashed strong white teeth. It lacked warmth. "One death dealer knows another."

Trixie tightened her hands into fists. *Death dealer.* No one had called her that, not since the lab.

"I don't deal in death." Not anymore.

"No?"

"No."

Bleary-eyed, hungry, and threatened, Trixie struggled with indecision. With the stranger's intense watching, she wanted nothing more than to bolt, to run—or burn the entire place down to the ground.

The latter sounded much better. She'd show them death. Inside her, the *other* voice that wanted to ignite the very tattered fibers of the world and watch it be devoured by her fury and outrage awoke. Her palms itched and she uncurled her hands, raising them.

Yes, she would show them all how to frighten, to harass with power, to be victims, like so many of her people had been victims—of dogs, chains, whips, spitting, beatings, lynchings...and police-sanctioned murder.

"Let's push on, sis." Fox whispered behind her.

Fox.

The fact he remained, standing beside, and depending on her, wrenched her back from the edge. He forced her fury to recede.

She thought of rising on new wings. They were above petty revenge. Freedom awaited.

Trixie swallowed the acidic taste on her tongue and backed away from the man. He remained standing, his pink face shining as if he were sweating hard. His bulk. His voice. His unrelenting stare had nothing on the creepiness and the iciness of his smile.

And he kept grinning as she stepped through the chapel's door.

Once outside, Fox yanked up his hood. "What the hell?"

"Let's just go." Trixie started toward the mountains again. "We need to find some food."

Death dealer.

She hadn't heard that term in, well, since the first time they'd escaped from the lab. Death trailed them, like a powerful and expensive perfume that lingered in the room once you'd already left. The bodies in their wake hadn't all been their fault. Still, it lingered in her. The redheaded nurse kept screaming as the lab burned around them, her hair aflame, and her eyes wide with agony...*death dealer.*

Trixie shuddered.

"You all right, Trix?" Fox came over to her.

"Yeah. Fine." She tried to put the memory away, but the woman's screams echoed deep into her psyche. Phoenix would burn it out. Then she'd stop hearing them. Now, the desert quiet amplified the memories. "We've got to get to the city. Get food. Get water."

In the faraway distance the metallic and mirrored city buildings reflected the sunlight and sparkled. A new day lumbered on. Trixie shook her head as the heat raged around them. They'd never make it walking, not in this heat. Her legs kept moving forward despite the truth in her logic.

The chapel grew smaller and smaller behind them. No one had come after them. It felt strange. So many had chased them. Followed them around stores, around neighborhoods, and around the lab.

Watching. Just like that man in the robe.

Most of her life Trixie had known only three things: Struggle. Fight. Run.

Despite the danger that wearing hoods invoked, they had yanked them on. It made it hot. Sure, it deflected some of the sun's rays, but the fabric had been crafted for colder climates. They'd gotten them in Flagstaff.

"Who was that guy?" Fox asked, his face partially shielded by his hood.

"Dunno." Trixie kept walking.

"He knew us." Fox shouted.

"He knew our *names*." Trixie added.

"More than we got on him, huh?" Fox looked at her and with a shrug, turned back to the road.

"We need a ride." Trixie wanted to put as much distance

between her and the man as she could. Something about him left her unsettled. She hadn't come all this way to meet her death and neither had Fox.

———

W*eeks later*
Trixie crossed into Phoenix proper and the man in the cloak didn't follow. She watched through the sliver of window blinds, but nothing seemed amiss in the pristine, perfect days of life in paradise. Manufactured air pumped through the domed in metro area. The bustling city had been contained from urban sprawl. To Trixie's dismay, the rising bird had been caged.

Trixie stepped out of the adobe home she and Fox shared. Over the last two weeks, her alarm had lessened. They were settling into an uncomfortable, but not unpleasant, existence. Trixie struggled with the newness of it all. Clean streets. Free food rations. Air conditioning. No poverty. No politics.

"No peace," Fox remarked, spooking her from behind.

She closed the blinds. "What?"

He tapped his temple. "No peace in here."

"This place is perfect." Trixie gestured to the tranquil scene just outside the windows. "No violence. No trash. Quiet. Even the vehicles are hushed."

They'd been accepted into the city as prelims. Their citizenship relied on how they contributed to the overall progress.

Fox shifted. "Yeah. Too quiet. There's no laughter, talkin', or arguin'."

"You miss the noise? The conflict? The fighting?"

"No, but…"

"Then it's perfect."

He frowned. "The air has an aftertaste."

Trixie sighed. It did.

"So, it isn't perfect. What if I go out and yell?" Fox walked to the door. It hushed open.

"Fox. We been through this. Regulations. This is quiet time."

"My point."

With that, he retreated to his room, a tight triangle corner of their adobe. Once they became full citizens, they'd get a bigger space.

Trixie gazed out over the neighborhood from the open door.

"Ah, there you are." The voice slithered around the sidewalk's curve.

Two weeks he'd waited.

The Gringo.

She and Fox had discovered others who spoke of the pale cloaked man they'd met at the chapel, the one who had called himself a death dealer. He'd been called The Gringo, yet no one knew his real name—only his lethal punishment for people who dealt in death, an avenging angel of sorts.

"Your handiwork, excuse the pun, is stamped all over this sector, Trixie."

Trixie narrowed her eyes as he faced her. Her palms itched in anticipation. "What the hell do you mean?"

The Gringo laughed. "Don't you smell it? The fear your presence generates?"

"We'll call the police! Get out of here!" Fox took out his phone.

The man tossed a fireball at Fox. Trixie screamed and dove in front of the hurling flames. The heat blew through her, singeing her eyebrows, brushing her face.

She scrambled to her feet and set her own palms on fire. The Gringo had encroached on their yard. *Who is this guy?*

"The Gringo has powers!"

"No kidding!" Trixie leapt back into the door. It closed, slicing off the sound fight.

Fox panted a few feet away. Already his shape threatened to shift. His eyes glowed scarlet and his knuckles curled into the beginnings of paws.

"No, Fox!" She hurried to calm him. Across from the door, his serum sat on the table, amber liquid in capped syringes. Trixie snatched the cap off of one and slammed it into his buttocks.

He howled in alarm and raced off through the house.

Outside, the Gringo continued his assault. Glass shattered. The scent of burning vegetation wafted inside.

"What do you want?" she shouted through the open door.

Blue and red lights spilled in. The police had arrived.

"Citizens. Desist your use of powers," a disembodied voice commanded. Disrupting the sanctioned quiet time was a serious offense.

Trixie crawled over broken glass and shattered furniture, some still smoking.

She and Fox had been chased across the southwest. Hunted. Then it clicked. Him.

"Fox! We have to get out of here! Find the sanctuary and plead for amnesty."

Pressed against the wall, drenched in sweat, Fox's nose had elongated into a snout. He barked out. "What? Now?"

"The Gringo!"

Damn. The serum injection had come too late and he'd already begun to change. Trixie sprinted around the room, snatching up their few possessions and tossing them into her satchel. Her hands shook.

"The Gringo?"

Trixie stopped. "I—I didn't think he really existed. Urban legend. Vapors. Remember Denver?"

Denver had been before Flagstaff.

Clean streets. Hushed quiet during daylight hours. Domed paradise. She'd been a fool. A gullible fool.

Freedom.

Before she could explain, the front door blew off its track. The Gringo came in, grinning.

"Out! Out! Damn black spots!"

"Spots?" Fox barked as he shifted to a sizable red fox, losing all ability to speak.

"Stains on the lovely purity of this city. I will make it *clean*." The Gringo grinned and rapidly threw fireballs at them.

"Run Fox!" Trixie deflected the attack with fire of her own.

The Gringo moved fast and, before long, had her by the throat. He threw her outside and she slammed into the manufactured lawn. It flickered as the hologram program crashed, revealing a section of dark gray plasma screen.

"Worthless. Designer scientists' cheap experiments." The Gringo revealed as he grabbed both her wrists when she tried to defend herself.

"Run Fox!" she shouted again.

Overhead, crisp blue sky and lemonade sun rested in the heavens. When she looked closely, she could see small reflections against the clear dome. Picture. Perfect. So quiet. No peace.

"You sought freedom." He laughed.

Trixie screamed as his hands burned the flesh around her wrists. Agony wretched through her. He'd set her skin on fire. The burning flames funneling out of his palms and scurried up her arms.

"Yes! Scream out your pathetic soul. If you bastards have one."

Trixie collapsed as he let go. Had it all come down to this? The fight? The struggle? All in vain.

She pushed back with flames of her own, fire against fire with her body the battlefield. The Gringo's powerful flames roared, his hatred fueling.

Agony wore through her anger, leaving only emptiness. Her fire quieted as she slumped to the ground.

The Gringo's grin was wide and cold. "Die."

Trixie shivered as her flame retreated, worn down by the Gringo.

Then, ripping through the afternoon's polished peace, a fox howled in the distance.

Now, it was her turn to smile. Warmth came and grew hotter.

She didn't scream as the agony of fire crackled along her flesh, her hair, her sight.

For like a phoenix, Trixie would rise.

The End

SISTERS OF THE WILD SAGE

"But all I learned from love was how to shoot somebody who
outdrew 'ya."
--Leonard Cohen, *Hallelujah*

1911
New Mexico Territory

The burning sands of the New Mexican earth blew
across the windswept landscape, tickling the cattle's
fine hairs and bringing with it the odor of cow dung and
burnt wood. Sanderine wore her cowboy hat low over her
eyes to protect them from the wind's grit and the sun's glare.
She peered across the land, *their land,* squinting as she
watched her fat cows graze lazily in the bright sunlight. They
chewed slowly as if the flavorless grass tasted delicious and

they meant to savor every blade. She wouldn't rush them. Happy cows gave sweet milk and made tender beef.

This made their meats and milk different from their competitors. Keep the cows happy. If you did, they willingly gave of themselves until nothing remained. Sanderine and Luna embraced their sacrifices and valued them for their self-lessness. Sometimes, when the nights went on long and the owls hooted, Sanderine thought about the cows' plight and felt bad for leading them to slaughter. Did slave owners feel the same? Knowing that they sold the flesh and milk and *life* of people to earn a nickel? Did they sit up at night and think about the horror of making them black folks happy with scraps from the master's table and elevated positions like placements in the big house, just to earn some cash? Destroying families to help support their own?

Sanderine scowled. Black folks ain't cattle. We people, her momma used to declare at the dinner table. Over time it became their mantra and as the family moved west, it became their mission—to show that they were people, not possessions.

Not to mention, it was obvious that white folks didn't value black bodies above what they could milk from them. After all, they went to war to keep the chains on, destroying a country in the process.

On those dreary evenings, Sanderine would blink back from the flames, and return to herself with her momma's husky but thunderous declaration echoing in her ears. Then she'd be right as rain when she went out to wrestle up the cows.

Her cows.

In the distance she heard a wagon rattling along the trail that lead into town. Their ranch sat off a secluded road and straddled a couple of acres of land just outside the town's official limits, not close enough to town to not have to entertain their troubles, but close enough to hear about them.

As the wagons rumbled past, Sanderine adjusted her gun belt strapped around her wide, shapely hips, and the guns therein. Her daddy's guns. He'd brought them west with him, along with his family, after the war. They'd been passed down to Sanderine's brother, Willie, after their father died fighting a mountain lion who'd come too far into their territory. The mountain lion had died too, but that offered little comfort.

Willie had died fighting off two white men in a saloon over in El Paso. The problem started with the Anglos making passes and lurid comments at Willie's momma. Sanderine's momma. Momma. The men called him out. Her big brother went out to defend his momma's honor and show he didn't have a yellow belly. Two against one. A fool's gamble. Willie rolled the dice anyway.

After he'd been shot down like a dog in the street, Willie didn't have sense enough to die. His moaning and groaning and bleeding disturbed the mayor's supper so one of the men marched down the high street and shot Willie in the head. The meat wagon scooped him up like horse manure and hauled him away. Her momma's screaming rang in her ears for years after. Sometimes Sanderine woke up in a sweat, still hearing her momma's anguish.

Watching in horror, Sanderine's momma snatched up her and Luna and fled to a tiny little shack hanging on the outskirts of town. Later, when her momma had been too exhausted from travel, grief, and booze, Sanderine snuck out and headed back to town.

She went to get her brother's guns from the sheriff.

She remembered that afternoon as clear as the one unfolding in front of her now.

Skinny, but not athletic, and sweaty Sheriff Nathaniel Boyd Baker with a patchy beard and rancid breath met her at the door. He tipped back his dusty cowboy hat and leered down at her.

"Whatcha want girl?"

"My brother's guns." Sanderine didn't hesitate. "Law says I should have 'em."

"I'm the law 'round here, girl." He coughed out a chuckle. "You a little spitfire. Ain't ya."

She didn't answer. *The long, broken arm of human law.*

"That nigger that got shot down by Everett and James your brother?" Sheriff Baker turned around and walked back into the jail.

Sanderine followed him inside, but stopped at the front table. "His name's Willie."

The sheriff glanced at her over his shoulder. "'Eh?"

"The colored man's name, my brother's name, is Willie," Sanderine said, more than aware of the steel she put into those words. Willie had been doing an honorable thing. She wouldn't let the sheriff dishonor him by calling him out of his name.

Sheriff Baker nodded and went to a trunk. He bent down, opened it, and squatted before it. When he stood, he turned to face her and marched back to the front of the building. He placed the guns on the table, looked at Sanderine up and down, and laughed.

When he managed to catch a wheezy breath, he said, "Take 'dem guns, ya' little nigger. They best not try to kill no more white men. Ya hear, ya little bitch?"

Sanderine glared at the shiny badge on his chest and watched it tarnish in the hot Texas heat. She then looked back up at him, and the lewd smile on his face fell. The sheriff had a whole lot of words, but he didn't pick the right ones to use. That had always confused her. Anglos had access to all the reading in the world, but when they spoke, they many times chose the wrong ones. They got access to so many, why pick so poorly?

"Look it, Bobby. This nigger's mute. Funny. That Willie couldn't shut the fuck up. Got his ass killed." Sheriff Baker chuckled and spit out a dark stream of tobacco stained spit.

Bobby, his deputy, a young, beanpole of a boy, shuffled uncomfortably for he saw the expression on Sanderine's face and it unsettled him. It pleased her, but she didn't dare let the deputy or the sheriff see it. They'd be all too quick to extinguish it. No. She took the guns and walked backward out the opened door and into the now.

"Sista! Sista!"

Luna's sing-songy call to her broke through the horrid memory. Sanderine blinked back to the present. With her heart pounding and her death grip on the horse's reins, she pushed it all aside, and turned her horse to face Luna's direction.

Her brother's death didn't change her, but she knew she wasn't the same after it happened. Everything was different but fine.

Luna, her younger sister and lone remaining family, walked across the fields of buffalograss, yucca, and cacti, her long, brown broom skirt catching on the needles as she passed. On foot, her boots protected her feet and ankles, but nothing protected Luna's spirit. It glowed from her, shining as bright as any desert flower. In her wake, new grass sprouted, healthy and vibrant, as if produced from warmer, more fertile grounds.

Her sister's powers simply overflowed from time to time,

like water over a dam. Sanderine sighed at Luna's dangerous habit. When Luna let it flow from her, as she did now, Sanderine's nervousness increased. If people discovered Luna's ability, they'd use her up. If she refused to conjure for them, they'd kill her.

Neither of those options worked for Sanderine, so she told Luna to keep her powers hidden. Not to mention the conjuring weakened Luna's body. She ate a lot, but after conjuring Luna would often take to her bed and rest for days on end, unable to do more than eat and go to the outhouse.

"Luna! For the gods, shut the well," Sanderine shouted from her horse. She trotted over and met Luna at the midway point between their house and Sanderine's spot on the pasture.

Stunning, with her dark hair's tight curls reaching for the sun, forming a round halo of her hair, Luna turned heads. Lithe, happy, and beautiful, she already started snaring men's attention in town. Smooth, dark skin, full womanly body, it was all some of them could do not to launch themselves at her. If anyone came here hunting for a victim, they'd find themselves an early grave. No one messed with Luna. No one would take what she wasn't giving.

Luna reached her and laughed. "Oh! Sorry." She looked back in her wake and spied the trail of Buffalograss sprouts. "I bet the cows would like that grass."

Sanderine nodded, unable to stay upset with Luna. "You got to be careful. How many time I gotta tell you? We don't know who lookin' at us."

Luna pouted, but didn't argue. Instead, she crossed her arms like she did at six.

"Watch your footing," Sanderine gestured toward the cow patty, "before you stomp ya feet."

Luna shuffled around it and stuck her tongue out at her

before bursting into a sigh. "I wanna go into town today. Can I go?"

Sanderine looked out at the cattle spread out across their land. They'd have to shift them to the outer sections soon to give this patch a rest.

"You ain't goin' alone and I just got the cows out here," Sanderine said and turned back to look down at Luna from horseback.

"Zeke said he'd take me." Luna smiled, big and anxious, the way she did when she got excited about something. Already a greenish glow ebbed at the bottoms of her boots. Little leaves poked through the soil. If she wasn't careful, she'd conjure an oak tree.

"Luna..." Sanderine warned.

"You won't regret it," Luna plowed on. "Please, sista. I already consulted the spirit board."

Sanderine tipped her cowboy hat back to get a better look at her little sister. "You did what?"

"I asked the spirit board. It said today's okay to go into town." Luna shrugged. "Please."

"It's already after noon, Luna. Zeke's got chores I'm payin' him to do. You got chores too. We ain't got time to run around for fun. Work's gotta get done."

"Please, I will do all of my chores tomorrow." Luna stepped in front of her horse and stroked Maybell's mane.

"What's in town you need to do anyway?"

Luna's big brown eyes dropped to the ground. She toed the soil. "I just need to go."

"Tomorrow." Sanderine didn't like the fact that Luna didn't tell her straight out. The shifty behavior surprised her. Most of their time they'd be open and honest with each other. Sanderine walked the tightrope between being momma and being a sibling.

Luna opened her full lips to argue, but she shut her mouth without a word. Instead she nodded numbly, turned on her heels, and walked back the way she'd come.

This time nothing sprung in Luna's retreating wake.

———

The following morning Sanderine found Luna already dressed and mounted onto her horse, Midnight. Sanderine frowned as she held her housecoat about her body. "Luna?"

The sound of horses had awakened Sanderine, and she'd rushed out to the porch to see about the ruckus. Zeke approached the porch from the stable, already mounted on his horse too. Sanderine became aware of her state of undress and folded her arms over her housecoat.

"Hola!" Zeke, Sanderine's and Luna's father's oldest friend, offered in greeting. He waved a gloved hand at Sanderine. He wore his denim, long sleeved shirt and his cowboy hat. He kept his head shaved close, but his face bore a long, tightly-curled beard. Flashes of grey crept through the mass of black hair. Zeke's large, wide eyes took in all, or so it seemed to Sanderine. He had been much younger than her daddy, but Zeke and Willie been friendly, too.

"Hi hombre!" Luna said in greeting.

Somehow no matter how frantic the moment, when Zeke arrived, everything ground to a halt. He stole the enchanting landscape's beauty and everyone's attention. Tall, fit, and charismatic, Zeke worked as a hired cowboy and stable hand. Sanderine paid him a wage, and he did his chores, but the wind brought loose talk and whispers about the two women living with a single man, all colored folk, up at a ranch.

Out here, the urge to survive often eroded the habit of hate.

Sometimes it fed it and it grew like a wild sage.

"Miss Sanderine. Miss Luna," Zeke nodded in her direction. He adjusted himself in his saddle and offered Sanderine a warm smile.

"What you doin' here?" Sanderine managed above the wind.

"Miss Luna wants to go into town today. She said you said it was okay." He shot Luna a questioning look.

"I did. Why you wanna go?" Sanderine tried not to meet Zeke's burning gaze. He didn't terrify her. Quite the opposite. She feared what she found in those dark eyes. It frightened her more that she'd accept the unspoken offer of desire in them.

"She's a child. She wanna go see Frankie. Go to the carnival." Zeke shrugged as if everything he said was of no big deal at all. "Kids get restless, ya know? It gets lonely out here."

That last hit her like an arrow. Sanderine's head snapped back to him. With her heart speeding up at the mere suggestion, she managed a dry, "I see."

"I ain't a child. I'm eight and ten." Luna broke her silence. She'd conjured flowers for Midnight's thick mane, and braided them into his hair.

"Sorry Miss Luna. I didn't mean to speak outta turn." Zeke chuckled.

"That ain't how grown folks act. Still not talkin' to me, huh?" Sanderine asked. Luna had given her the silent treatment all evening the day before. "No breakfast? Coffee, Zeke?"

Luna shrugged her narrow shoulders. The thin fabric of her dress pulled taut against her. It had been their momma's, then Sanderine's, and now Luna's. She'd almost outgrown the thing.

Sanderine sighed. Both Zeke and Luna awaited her decision. Sanderine had promised herself and her momma, after the incident with the sheriff and the guns—to never again take unnecessary risks. They'd already lost the men in their family to violence at the hands of Anglos. She swore and fingered one of the pistols' barrels.

"I told you yesterday, Luna. Zeke's got chores." Sanderine looked at him to avoid watching Luna's crestfallen expression. Zeke blushed. "Maybe go tomorrow."

What is he and Luna up to anyway? They both look guilty.

"There's a carnival in town!" Luna blurted out.

"A carnival?"

"Yeah! Sista, they have tigers and lions and zebras! They leavin' tomorrow." Luna exclaimed. All around Midnight little pink flowers sprouted. She fidgeted and Midnight pranced about in an unsettled fashion. "We'll be back by dark."

Zeke grinned at her enthusiasm. "I took care of the horses and milked the cows earlier, miss."

"Earlier." Sanderine's eyebrows rose.

"Yes, ma'am. Miss Luna asked me yesterday. I wanted to be available to avoid a wall." Zeke explained in his deep, rumbling voice.

Sanderine peered at the two across from her. Zeke and Luna had been inseparable of late.

"Zeke, you 'member the frenzied attack outside Wild Sage about a week ago?" Sanderine asked, knowing full well he did. It had been the talk of the town for days.

"Yeah. Some thieves used brute force to steal Mr. Young's cows and a few horses," Zeke said. "A bloody mess."

"That's a dangerous business. So be sure my sister comes

back, alive. If she dies, you do, too, in the same manner as those poor folks." Sanderine said.

"Strong words, Miss Sanderine." Zeke sobered, his warm smile dissolved. "Like you, I stumbled through this world and I lost people I cared about and loved. I know what Miss Luna means to you. I will protect her."

"You speak to me in lies," Sanderine said, her heart pinched in angst. "I let you go on out with my family before, Zeke."

Zeke had found her daddy's body. The two were out hunting together, but only Zeke returned alive. Long ago now, but the injury left a scar, thick and raised along Sanderine's emotional surface.

"I won't let you down." Zeke huffed out a sigh.

"Again."

"No, not again, Miss Sanderine."

"! I can take care of myself," Luna interjected.

"Let's go, Zeke."

"I'm not satisfied with your say so, Luna," Sanderine said, her cheeks hot at her little sister's declaration.

"I don't care!" Luna shouted over her shoulder as she galloped off toward the ranch's gate.

"Luna!"

Frustration rendered Sanderine to tears. She started to follow, but Zeke barred her with his arm.

"She a thorn in your side, but you can't keep her caged forever." Zeke trotted closer to Sanderine. "I *will* bring her back by nightfall."

Sanderine met those warm eyes, but her nerves remained on alert. "You better."

"I love the light in your eyes when you get all mad," Zeke shouted as he galloped after Luna, leaving Sanderine furious.

She watched them until they disappeared over the horizon.

———

I *can't breathe.*
Luna sucked in a huge, lungful of air to prove they still worked. She'd never used such strong words with Sista. Today, she used her voice and spoke up, but Luna knew her momma spun in her grave at her actions. Sista basically raised her and led their family after Willie died. Momma told them stories of life in Tennessee. At first, they sounded horrible, but what Luna learned of life was that it didn't care about coloreds. It snuffed folks out in their prime of joy. Luna wouldn't wait until it happened to her. She meant to live the life.

Hooves drumming against the earth interrupted her musings.

"You owe Miss Sanderine your respect," Zeke called out to her, once he caught up. His stern expression melted, and so did his tone. "She worried about you."

Luna sighed. She remembered Sista's shocked and hurt face. Her cold bitterness warmed to shame. She glanced at the path unfolding in front of them.

"I know."

The sun sat high in the sky. Luna wore her floral scarf tied over her hair, but the blazing sunlight hurt her eyes. A gila monster raced across the route, probably crossing to avoid trouble.

Zeke didn't lecture her about her actions. Yeah, she and Sista were perturbed with each other, but Zeke understood that. They rode on in silence. She spied Zeke's gunbelt and the pistols strapped there.

"Thank you." Luna called to Zeke's broad back.

He nodded and turned his cowboy hat before putting his attention back on their surroundings. She snapped the reins and Midnight galloped up to him.

"It ain't my fault we live all the way out here." Luna hoisted her chin up.

"This desolate spot of farmland was hard to get," Zeke explained, but his eyes remained locked on the shadows ahead where the path bent. "Your daddy gave his life for that land."

"You were his friend." Luna smiled. She'd known Zeke most of her whole life. Was he concealing something now? He seemed distant.

"He was like a daddy to me," Zeke said, his tone suddenly softer. It held sadness the way canteens held water.

"I wish I would've gotten a chance to know him," Luna said. Desert flowers bloomed at Midnight's feet as they traveled. "I only 'member bits and pieces."

"Hush!" Zeke jerked the reins of his horse. The horse halted. So did Luna and Midnight. He raised his pistol in his other hand in the air before aiming in at a spot in front of them. "Close your eyes!"

"Why?" Luna searched around the area. Her heart beat faster.

"Just do it!" Zeke hissed.

Midnight didn't like it, but Luna didn't either. She shut her eyes, but as she did, her hearing sharpened. She heard grunting and mumbling. Peering through her half-opened lids, she spied Zeke a short distance away, dismounted and inching toward something on the ground. His pistol remained trained on the horror in front of them. She saw his jaunty motions and then looked ahead to see what frightened him.

A grim scene came into view with each step forward. Trembling with nerves, Luna fought to keep from screaming when her mind figured out what it was. On the ground, a heap of charred bones and flesh sat in the road's center. Blood splattered the sandstone and neighboring brush. It dried and melded along the desert's browns.

She gasped.

Zeke heard her. "I told ya! Close ya eyes!"

"I seen butchered cows." Luna inched Midnight closer. "I ain't afraid of blood."

"It ain't the same when it a person, girl." Zeke held his arm out to keep her from moving forward. "Don't be in a hurry to throw ya life away."

"I'm not," Luna ignored his rebuke. She fought down the churning in her belly. It was hard to describe the smell of rotting human flesh. The pungent odor mixed with the burning of skin and it all reeked. "It looks strange."

"Cause that ain't all of him" Zeke held his hand up to his nose and waved her back with his free hand.

Luna scanned the area and spied the person's head a few feet behind some wildflowers. Zeke couldn't see it from his position. It had a big hole in the back of it. Tremendous hack marks on his face and jaw marred the full picture of what he might've looked like. The head still had flesh on it, despite this. Brown skin. Dark brown skin.

Colored.

Another colored body broken by violence. Whoever did this left him, robbing him of his valuables and his life, the ultimate theft.

Anger sparked inside her to lose someone in such a useless way, becausesomeone's desperate and prone to violent behavior. She thought of his people who missed him, worried about him. She swallowed the bitter outrage in her heart. *How dare they leave him here like this!* Hacked apart and cooked by flame like an animal.

He was a man.

A colored man.

From the looks of it, his eyes had been chopped out. Had he dared to look at his attackers in the face? Did it remind them of his humanity, so they destroyed it?

Luna dismounted from her horse propelled by outrage.

"What you doin'? Get back on Midnight!" Zeke ordered. His worry turned to panic. He shouted at her instead of the previous guarded whispers. "Bandits do this to lure folks to they death!"

To Luna, Zeke's words came from the end of a long cave.

She looked around for witnesses, and walked toward the corpse with her hand outstretched. Zeke snatched her arm. He'd crept up to her, startling her with his fast movement. She hadn't seen him move.

"What the hell ya doin'?" His lips were a slash of annoyance.

"I ain't gonna be denied." Luna shook him off. "This was a person..."

"He dead. Like us if we don't get movin'."

"No! I ain't gonna leave him here like this, in the dirt." Luna balled up her fists and held Zeke's furious gaze.

"You can't help 'em, Miss Luna," Zeke said, his voice rising in pitch.

Luna elbowed by him, stretched out her hand and closed her eyes. She called forth the grass, pulling from the earth's energies and accelerating them with her own. She conjured the magic inside her, the energy in her blood, and fed it to the hungry plants beneath the ground. In moments, blades plowed through the dirt and pushed eagerly toward the sunlight. The vegetation sped across the blackened body, crawling over it until it covered him. Once it resembled a grassy mound with a few flowers, Luna pulled her arms against her chest. She stumbled, but Zeke raced to catch her before she fell to the ground. Dizzy, Luna wobbled, but she let Zeke help her back onto Midnight.

"You a fool Miss Luna," Zeke whispered.

"Now he can't be used to ambush others," Luna said, words slurred together. The magic had almost taken all she had. "They. Can't. Use 'em."

They started home.

"Your eyes glow when you do that," Zeke said, voice soft against the now still air, "You a heavenly sight, Miss Luna."

"That's one way of putting it," Luna said before blood spurted out of her mouth and all over Midnight's mane.

"God!" Zeke scrambled to check on her. He lifted her head. "Luna?"

"Yeah," Luna said, but everything felt so heavy.

Luna gave him a bloodied grin before passing out.

———

A violent thunderstorm rumbled off in the distance, filling the tense silence surrounding Sanderine. Her skin prickled at the electricity in the air. The cattle mooed in restlessness, perhaps sensing the tension and unsettled weather. She hadn't taken them out far today to graze, and she rounded them up sooner than they were probably ready. Her gun belt hung from one of the two chairs, but Sanderine still felt a weight on her. Their house didn't look tidy, but it also wasn't unkept. Two women lived there, but one would not know it from observing the living quarters.

Outside, she leaned against one of the porch beams. She hoped Zeke didn't come back in a sodden condition. The man did like his drink. How foolish had she been to let Luna go to a carnival? Only freaks and snake oil salesmen prowled those places. She'd been swayed by Zeke's silky words. Luna did whatever floated into her mind. Always had, and most of the time, Sanderine could corral her. Not today.

Outside, the clouds darkened the heavens. Somehow, perhaps when she kept her eyes on their ranch, Luna had crested into adulthood, and Sanderine didn't want to eclipse her. A nervous crawling blanketed her. Sanderine only saw her little sister, and it didn't match the fiery independent woman in her house. The terrain wasn't the only dangerous thing out here in the West.

A glint caught her meandering attention. It traveled fast as if spurned on by the devil. Sanderine raced inside, claimed one of her pistols, and hurried back out to the porch. She'd have more leverage on horseback. Without pondering it further, she ran to the stables. In a flurry, she untethered her horse, Maybell. She didn't bother with a saddle, and hoisted herself up on the horse with the strength of her arms and Maybell's leaning down for her to clear her back.

A pistol in hand, she wrapped her other hand in Maybell's mane. With her heels and a loud, "Ha!" they bolted out of the stable to greet the coming threat. Maybell's hooves thundered as they rode.

"By the ancestors," Sanderine prayed, her heart matched the frantic pace. Whomever had come out to her home best be ready to die if their intentions weren't pure.

Ahead the silhouettes merged as she got closer, but then separated in the lightning's illumination. Luna's floral scarf glowed in the darkened day and caught her attention. Sanderine sped up, terror in her throat.

"Luna!" Her next thought was *Zeke?* Where the hell was Zeke?

Then the other person came into view, larger, wearing a cowboy hat, and riding a dark horse.

"Zeke!"

Once she reached them, breathless and panicked, Sanderine looked at her sister draped over Midnight. The dark and dried blood splatter matted on the horse's neck and in his hair. It raised her alarm.

The pistol appeared in her fist before she could blink. "Luna? What's wrong with her? Why is there blood here?"

"Whoa! I'm on your side, Miss Sanderine. She's fine. She's alive." Zeke spoke slowly and he stayed still.

"She don't look fine." Sanderine's eyes burned in fury. She knew it! She shouldn't have let him take her baby sister to a carnival.

"She asleep. Look at her!" Zeke pleaded with a nod to Luna's body.

Swallowed by doubt, all she saw was Luna's limp condition. Her finger slipped onto the gun's trigger. "I trusted you."

"She. Alive." Zeke repeated, eyes wide with fear. "I promise."

At his shout, Luna started to shake and cough on the horse beside him. She lifted her head, swayed, and said, "Sista?"

Sanderine's heart swelled, squeezing out her anger. "Luna!"

She dropped her pistol to her side. *She's alive.* Then fled to her sister's side. She pushed the plastered and sweaty hair from her forehead. Dried blood around her mouth and her damp forehead spoke to Luna's ill state.

"You almost took my head off!" Zeke exclaimed, relaxing in his saddle. "Your eyes said you'd kill me."

"I've got potential to do that very thing," Sanderine said to him. "What happened to her?"

Zeke hunched against the wind. "Can we go inside? It gonna rain. We need to get Luna inside."

Sanderine climbed off her horse. She shoved her pistol into the small of her back. With her hands free, she reached across Midnight for Luna. She felt her sister's damp face. Slightly warm. She'd seen Luna like this before.

"She been conjuring. Too much for the looks of it. Damn it." Sanderine took Midnight's reins and started back to their home. "Better not have been at that carnival."

"No, not there. I'll tell ya when we get inside." Zeke hopped down and took Maybell's reins along with his horse's own pair.

Lightning cracked the sky.

Moments later the sky rumbled in complaint.

The darkened sky opened up and rain poured down onto the lands. It drummed on the roof, threatening to drown out Sanderine's shouting at his antics. Luna lay in her bed, tucked in by her big sister, and left to recover. Sanderine returned to the living space and the central fire place, pacing back and forth. Zeke stood close to the fire and its robust flames. Though he still could get burned, not by the fire, but by Sanderine's fury.

Her response to him taking Luna off the ranch had been met with her legendary fiery temper.

"She an adult," Zeke said with his hands resting on his own hips.

"She let a friend convince her to go to a carnival! She's hardly an adult, Zeke." Sanderine threw her hands up before they came to rest on her shapely hips. "She needs to gain control of her conjuring."

"It seems to me, Miss Sanderine, she got a good handle on

it." He crossed his arms crossed over the wide expanse of his chest.

"I dunno why I even let her go with you." Sanderine swore.

"Why? I'm family." Zeke stepped closer to her.

Sanderine glared. "You ain't family. You just like a stranger working here collectin' a wage."

Zeke flinched and stared at her. Sanderine marched off toward the door. She stared out into the pouring rain.

"That's harsh. Sometimes you can find comfort in strangers. You would if you quit bein' so stubborn."

"Stubborn? I'm protectin' my sister." Sanderine spun around to face him. He'd poked a sore spot, and she'd come up fighting.

Zeke sighed. "What did I do wrong?"

Sanderine's eyes bucked. "You dunno? Luna…"

Zeke waved that off. "No. Not that. You're not mad at me about Luna. Ya mad cause I lovin' ya with my whole heart. Imma follow ya my whole life, Miss Sanderine, and ya can be as angry as ya want, but Imma keep love ya."

Sanderine's mouth slacked at his comments. She snatched herself away and swallowed hard. In her tiny home, there were limited places to flee. Zeke followed her, tight on her heels. She could smell him, his scent, filling the space around her. She turned away from him, her hair, braided in two long plaits on either side of her head, partially shielded her face. The fireplace burned on, casting shadows onto the walls.

"I'm not bein' rude, but ya attitude is ruinin' every day I'm here. Ya got me tied 'round ya finger, Miss Sanderine. Imma fool for ya, but I do wish ya attitude would change."

"My attitude?" Sanderine repeated. She faced him full out.

Zeke threw up his hands in surrender. "The minute I came here, I knew I wasn't gonna leave, 'cause I love ya."

"And my daddy. He know ya feelins' 'bout me and my attitude?"

Zeke blew a slow breath. "He did. I told him that day, 'bout how I wanted to marry ya."

"You lie!" She studied his face.

The truth shone from those dark, warm eyes. For all of her fussing, she didn't often find Zeke to be telling tales. He'd told her daddy of his love for her, and now, she could see it shining out from his face.

"I ain't lyin'," he said.

In slow motion, Zeke guided her into his embrace and held her. Zeke's arm felt good wrapped around her shoulder. So much happened in her life she'd forgotten how it felt before the world of responsibility fell at her feet. She melted into his embrace, allowing her rigid wall to crumble just a bit.

"If ya don't love me, ya need to say," Zeke whispered against the top of her head.

Sanderine wanted to scream aloud at the smothering of it all. The newfound knowledge of Zeke's love for her threatened to overwhelm her. She slowly sank into his arms, but she couldn't sort out her feelings.

"Gimme time."

"Forever," Zeke said, "But I'll leave ya with ya misery."

One thing Sanderine did know with certainty—hearts are broken every day out here in the harsh and often unforgiving land and wilderness.

"You can't hold me together, Zeke. I got to stand on my own. That's all I know."

He stroked his beard. "I know."

Time stilled as it often did when Zeke came around. She untangled herself from him, and went to stand at the door, listening to the wind whip the rain against the house. The fire crackled and popped as water droplets sizzled as they came down the chimney.

She heard him sink into one of the two rocking chairs that sat around the fireplace. The creaking commenced. In minutes, the pipe's tobacco wafted over to her, enveloping her in its embrace.

Sanderine felt so far from where she'd been just this morning.

———

J ust after the sun broke over the horizon the following morning, Luna bolted upright in her bed, spooking Sanderine, in the neighboring twin bed, into doing the same. With wide eyes, Luna threw back the blankets and scrambled out of bed. She pushed her feet into her boots, and hurried out of the room.

"Luna? Luna! What's going on?" Sanderine pushed her blankets off, snatched her robe, and rushed after her sister. "Stop! Tell me what's happenin'!"

In the living space, Zeke jerked awake from his seated position in the rocking chair. He clutched his pistols to him and drew them. He blinked several times, forcing himself awake, and tried to figure out why Sanderine had started shouting. When she raced by him, he sprung to his feet and followed, keeping his guns at the ready.

"Miss Sanderine?" he asked, his alarm slipped through the thick tension now packed into their kitchen.

Luna came to a halt at the door, with her hands in fists and her hair illuminating in an eerier green color. Around her booted feet, vines sprouted and commenced snaking up her ankles. Otherwise, she appeared fine.

214

Confounded, Sanderine touched Luna's shoulder. "Luna?"

"We got company," Luna said and nodded to something outside the door. "A swarm of horseback heathens encroaching on our lands."

Zeke guided her behind him, tripping over the vines, and took a look for himself. He stood in the door's center, blocking the two women from seeing out. He gave a long whistle.

"How many?" Sanderine asked, putting on her gun belt around her housecoat. No time for changing clothes.

"Ten, maybe a bit more in the back." Zeke answered. He frowned at the line of men on horseback just outside the fence's closing. They flanked the leader, clad in dusty denims, filthy with mud from yesterday's rain. Even from this distance, Zeke made him out. "Everett Boone."

"Everett." Sanderine paused.

Zeke nodded.

"I'm going out there," Luna said.

"You'd be swallowed up by that throng of people," Sanderine cautioned, her hand on Luna's shoulder. "We need a plan."

"They ain't here to raise the dead," Zeke said over his shoulder. "They here for land or Luna."

"What do you mean, for Luna?" Sanerine spun around in surprise to him.

Zeke scratched his beard with the back of his hand, fingers still curled around the gun. "She conjured out in the open yesterday. Somebody could've seen her."

Sanderine swore. "This here is our land. We ain't 'bout to be pushed off it and they damn sure ain't gettin' Luna."

"I ain't useless," Luna said, her eyes narrowed in

anger. "I won't be made idle by despair. I got a right to live like I wanna."

"Now, Miss Luna, you 'member what they did to that other person." Zeke spoke in a calm, matter of fact tone. "These here men ain't playin'."

"My hands may be small, but they will cause big hurt," Luna replied. "I 'member well what they did."

"I dunno what's gotten into you, Luna, but this could get bad fast." Sanderine put a sheathed blade into her boot.

"That's a little thing," Zeke said, nodding at Sanderine's boot.

"Small knife wounds cause big damage," Sanderine said, looking at him with dead calm.

"Ya gotta get close to do real damage," Zeke warned, concern wrinkling his face.

"This *is* personal. You come onto my land and try to take my sister. Oh yeah, it's gonna get close," Sanderine explained.

"Ya gonna put on some clothes?" Zeke asked. He averted his gaze from her, and back to the looming threat outside.

"My ancestors fought nude, maimed, beaten, and barefoot with their belly and breasts bare to defend what was theirs, their kin, and their lives," Sanderine said, and pushed by Zeke on out to the porch. "I'm overdressed."

She and Luna stepped out onto the porch. Zeke came behind them, his pistols ready, one in each hand. Sanderine met Luna's eyes and they both nodded at the same time. Over the years, they had dealt with several attacks against them, their cattle, or their property. Not one this size, of course, but they had a well-used plan for addressing threats. Zeke had missed those incidents due to a variety of reasons. Some men think without a male at their property, women would be easier to defeat.

Those individuals were buried on the property or pushing up daisies somewhere else with the foolhardy.

Zeke whistled low. "Don't throw your lives away for some meaningless land."

"This land is meaningful to me," Luna said hands outstretched, fingers splayed.

"I done told you. We ain't givin' up." Palm sweat made gripping a challenge, but Sanderine's unnatural talent lay in her hands, like Luna's. While her little sister conjured life, Sanderine called forth death. Her guns never missed. Ever.

"Get out here woman!" Everett shouted above the gentle morning breeze. "I can break your silence."

"He can try." Sanderine scowled and clenched her teeth as she stepped down from her porch.

Zeke blanched. "He want the land, Sanderine. It ain't worth your life or Luna's."

"I'd watch it burn before the likes of Everertt Boone get his hands on it," Sanderine said.

Zeke snatched her arm. "I'm serious. Take these guys seriously."

"I ain't ready to make nice." Sanderine shook him off. "See, Luna and I ain't normal God's creatures. Luna conjures. I never miss. You can say we a family of means."

Zeke scratched his beard with his overhand palm. With an unsettled look, he said, "Huh?"

"Just watch and don't get killed."

Luna pretended not to notice. They didn't have time.

Sanderine stepped off the porch and made a beeline for her gate with Luna on her heels. She thought to get her horse, but it would take too much time. She wanted this done and over with. Cows needed milking and their garden needed tending.

Across from her, Everett Boyd leaned on his saddle's handle at her approaching with a wide, leering grin. His body language said he found the whole thing amusing and fun. As they marched toward him, Everett gave into a tremendous amount of coughing. When he regained his composure, he spat out a hunk of phlegm onto the ground just as Sanderine and Luna reached the gate.

"Must be the stench in the air," he said, wiping his mouth with the back of his sleeve.

His cronies laughed.

"Newcomers got a certain smell. Filth," Everett said to Sanderine.

His arms bore defensive wounds in the fabric, across his face and hands, too. These men met and survived violence. Everett took out his hunting knife from its sheath. The blade scraped across his gun's barrel. He had the pistol in one hand and his knife in the other. One of the men beside him started throwing punches in the air, demonstrating what he intended to do to her or Zeke.

"Leave us in peace, Everett. You got no interest here." Sanderine wrapped her hands around her pistols. "Get on now."

Everett laughed, the way he had at Willie. "I don't take orders from coloreds. I come for the girl with the magic. Imma be leavin' with her too. But you ain't got nothin' special, so you better run faster than my bullets," he warned with a sneer twisting his lips in a cruel expression. "Or end up like your brother."

"You ain't gettin' either. You gonna leave here disappointed." Sanderine raised her guns.

"Ya can't hide her from the light of day," Everett leered.

"Sweet lil treasure like that. We gonna have her." Once his crew stopped grunting their approval, he pointed his gun at Sanderine. "Ya hear?"

With a vengeance, Sanderine fired. Like pins, men around Everett fell from their horses, clutching their chests or other parts of their torso. A few had nice, clean holes in their heads.

Luna launched her assault in tandem with her sister. All around the horses' feet vines sprouted from the dirt and with thirsty speed raced up the beasts' legs and the men's too, entangling them before they could fire or fire or flee. Soon, the vines covered their faces, essentially cocooning them in vegetation.

"Rise above the mess!" Sanderine shouted to Luna as she leapt behind one of the wooden fence posts. It didn't provide a ton of cover, but it gave her something. "Rise!"

She didn't know where Zeke had gotten off to. She didn't know if he'd even made it off the porch, so focused she'd been on Everett, who as of now lay slumped over his horse.

Sanderine saw several of the men doing the same. Less than had ridden out to her ranch to begin with. It pleased her to see them retreat, but it scared her too. Would they send more people to attack under the guise of arresting them? She trained her gun on one of the men, still seated on horseback but rooted to the spot by Luna's vines, gargling as the plant squeezed the breath from his body. Sanderine sighed and fired. A perfect bullet hole appeared in the center of his forehead. He twitched once before becoming still.

Although many deserved it, she didn't like to see them suffer. She listened to the silence, inhaled the odor of gunpowder, and horse manure and blood. It ended as soon as it had begun and that pleased her. Luna's conjuring came with a toll. The longer she had to use it, the longer it would take for her to recover.

Sanderine stepped out from behind the fence post. A silence had descended on the ranch. No moaning or groaning, for life had fled, leaving only husks of men. She spied Luna on her knees on the ground. She fell forward, but caught herself with her arms. With her head bowed, her arms trembling, and blood vomiting from her mouth, Luna couldn't call for help.

The gruesome scene frightened Sanderine. She put her guns in their holster, and hurried to her sister. *Where the hell was Zeke?* All the men had fled, thinking this would be easy, and learning it wasn't, cost some of them their lives, and the others had gained a newfound knowledge.

Sanderine dropped beside Luna and scooped her sister into her arms. She'd gotten so swept up in defeating Everett, she'd lost track of Luna during the battle. They'd never faced that many men before. She swore at her selfishness and held her sister close.

"Luna! Luna!"

Luna opened her eyes, but only just. She swallowed with difficulty and she had blood around her mouth. "Sista?" Her eyes couldn't seem to focus. Her skin was cold to the touch, and she lacked strength.

"You with me?" Sanderine asked, gently. "I need you here, little moon. I'd miss our talks if you left me now."

Luna gave her an open mouth grin. "So. Tired."

"Rest. You earned it." Sanderine kissed her forehead.

"Did. We. Win?"

"Yes, we did."

At this Luna relaxed, her body became limp in Sanderine's arms. Her chest rose and fell.

But only once more.

———

A *Month Later*

Sanderine came out to stand on the porch, greeting the rising sun. She flinched at its brightness. Everything seemed darker with Luna dead, thus the sunlight hurt. She would take strength in her pain and push on. The scars on her heart hadn't healed, and Sanderine had realized early own it was foolish to think they would.

The life she had with Luna had been left behind, a cold and empty room of memories and regret Sanderine often returned to visit, each night she set about to rest.

"A memory and a ghost is all that I have left of my family," she said to the wind.

In return, a warm summer wind blew the sweet scent of buffalograss across the land and her face. It made her smile.

Zeke emerged from the stables. "How ya doin, Miss Sanderine?"

"I'm half alive, but I feel mostly dead," Sanderine croaked, lifting her head up to meet his shifty gaze.

Zeke grimaced. "I'm gonna move the cattle to the far end today. They like the grass there the best. That okay?"

Sanderine nodded. Of course they liked that grass the best. It was close to where Luna had been buried.

An hour later, the cows moaning rose like a chorus against the cornwall blue New Mexican sky. Sanderine stood up from her rocking chair and turned toward Luna's grave. She wrapped her hand around the wooden handle of her pistol and set out to chase off a coyote or a wolf hanging around the weaker herd members.

As Sanderine crested the slightly inclined land, she came

to an abrupt halt. Floating above her grave, her skin verdant and green as vibrant grass, Luna reached out to her. Vines held her firm, not in restraint, but in support.

She'd finally learned to master her gift.

Sanderine hesitated but a moment, before racing full out to greet her sister.

"Luna! Luna!" she shrieked, not sure if she'd given in to madness or she'd been blessed. Neither mattered.

Once she reached Luna, her younger sister smiled sweetly down to her as the vegetation that obeyed her, lowered her to the lush ground.

"Hello Sanderine," Luna said, her hair a bush filled with flowers. Her purple eyes and green-hued lips broke into a smile. "I've missed you."

Sanderine snatched Luna into her arms. "I thought I lost you."

Luna hugged her back. "I'm a part of the land. As long as you live here, I will be also."

"Forever." Sanderine wept.

"Forever." Luna promised. "This is our land. Always."

The End

ABOUT THE AUTHOR

Nicole Givens Kurtz's short stories have appeared in over 40 anthologies of science fiction, fantasy, and horror. One of her favorite destinations is the West, particularly the Southwest. Her novels have been finalists for the EPPIEs, Dream Realm, and Fresh Voices in science fiction awards. Her work has appeared in Bram Stoker Finalist, *Sycorax's Daughters*, and in such professional anthologies as Baen's *Straight Outta Tombstone* and Onyx Path's *The Endless Ages Anthology*.

Visit Nicole's other worlds online at Other Worlds Pulp, www.nicolegivenskurtz.com.

41134425R00144

Made in the USA
San Bernardino, CA
30 June 2019